Pierce-Arrow
Publishing

WANTED DEAD

The Legend of Henry Berry Lowrie

By
Warren R. Reichel

WANTED DEAD

The Legend of Henry Berry Lowrie

2nd Edition

ACKNOWLEDGMENTS

This book would not have been possible without the encouragement and help of my friends and family. I especially wish to thank my editor, Jackie Rosenfeld, who never gave up hope.

My proof-readers, who doggedly worked to find all the mistakes I'd inadvertently made. These are my best friends and family: Robert Manfred Schmitt, Heidi Flythe, Frieda, and Richard McMaster, Roberta "Kato" Fountain, and Matt Sandy.

I'd also like to thank Susan Avery for taking the snapshot used in the *About the Author* section of this book.

All of you should know how much I appreciate your assistance, candid, honest comments, and friendship.

Thank you.

150TH ANNIVERSARY!

(2015 – 2022)

… the **150th anniversary** of what was known to the citizens of Robeson County, North Carolina, as

"The Lowrie War."

(1865 -1872)

WANTED DEAD
The Legend of Henry Berry Lowrie

...tells the story of those seven years Known as **The Lowrie War**;

which turned a local Hero, and his Band-of-Brothers,

into a

LEGEND.

Adjusted for inflation
$300 of 1865 dollars
is worth **$4,494** in 2018

Warren R. Reichel

Adjusted for inflation
$2,000 of 1870 dollars
is worth **$36,614** in 2018

Adjusted for inflation
$10,000 of 1871 dollars
is worth **$196,733** in 2018

Adjusted for inflation
$20,000 of 1871 dollars
is worth **$393,466** in 2018

Adjusted for inflation
$40,000 of 1872 dollars
is worth **$786,931** in 2018

WANTED DEAD

The Legend Of Henry Berry Lowrie

1865

In these here parts, if you ain't white, you got no rights.

Pollie Lowrie

Total documented raids on local plantations by the Lowrie Gang
in **1865 = 12**

CHAPTER 1

January 1

The small train depot was crowded with people anxiously awaiting the arrival of the midday train, which most of them anticipated would deliver family and friends. Such a gathering at this depot was unusual. However, since the fall of Fort Fisher and the Port of Wilmington, Southerners were fleeing westward, ahead of the advancing Yankee armies.

Unseen to those around the station were two young men standing just inside the tree-line shadows. The older of the two was seventeen years old; his friend was fourteen. The boys were like most any other boy of that time. They were average height; wore contemporary clothing and were styled like most men of the era. Both men were Indians, and both were trying to grow beards, though there was still much filling-in needed in places. The younger man had broad shoulders and was stocky from a lifetime of manual labor. The older teen was lean with sinewy muscles that were toned and taut. His features made him appear more cavalier than rugged. His grandfather had called him a "yerker," which, in their language, means *mischievous child*. He had blue eyes that were rivaled only by the Carolina blue skies on a sunny day. When he was happy and laughing, his eyes would light up a room. His name was Henry Berry Lowrie. He and his best friend, Boss Strong, were waiting for the train to meet Boss's mother, Cee, and his older sister, Rhoda.

The young men weren't in the shadows playing games; they needed to see who was around the depot and The Settlement ("Scuffletown" by white vernacular), which included a couple of shops and a bar. The young men knew they could be arrested by members of the Home Guard for avoiding service as needed by the

Confederate Army, which meant digging trenches and fortifications. As non-citizens, they weren't allowed to fight in the army because, by law, they weren't allowed to own guns. And, even though it looked like the war was going to be over, a bounty could still be collected on them or worse they could be shot dead because of *trying to escape.* This possibility was all too real for not six months ago, two of Henry's cousins had been shot "trying to escape" while being transported back to work at Fort Fisher.

Some whites even joked that maybe being shot was a better way to die than dying in agony from the *Yellow Jack*, a term for the victims of Yellow Fever because their skin would turn a yellowish color. And, once a person turned yellow, they could expect to cough up their bloody lungs and die within three days. The "sooner the better" was preferred over such suffering.

So many died from working in the coastal marshlands that slave owners refused to send any more of their slaves to work on the fortifications. That was the reason the Home Guard had looked to fill the manpower shortage with local Indians. The problem was the local Indians around Lumberton and Maxtown wouldn't cooperate. They'd all gone deep into the swamps where the Home Guard couldn't find them.

With the fall of Fort Fisher, not only were the Yankees occupying Wilmington, but news had arrived that Sherman's Army had taken the Port of Savannah. This meant the South was being eviscerated and would die from her wounds.

Therefore, it seemed unlikely the Home Guard would harass anyone at this point in the war. However, it was wise for the Indians never to forget that these were white men, and there was no telling how they might react. Better to avoid them, which was why Boss and Henry Berry shied away within the shadows.

The two were anxious for the train's arrival. They'd not seen Boss's mother or sister since they left two years earlier to take care of their old grandmother. They left in part to get away from the harassment of the Home Guard, but mostly because it was a tradition for a nubile young woman to stay with an old Indian woman to learn how to be a housewife, mother, cook, and nurse. It was a time to learn lessons passed down from their people.

The last time the men had seen Rhoda, she was wearing britches and ponytails. And, even though Henry enjoyed Rhoda's company, at times he and the other men felt she was just a kid hanging around and trying to keep up. But Rhoda had secretly always had a crush on Henry Berry and dreamed she'd marry him someday.

Finally, clouds of steam could be seen rising above the tree line, and soon the sound of the train's whistle announced the approaching train and its cargo of passengers.

Once the train had come to a full stop, passengers began to disembark. Henry and Boss didn't see anyone they felt would cause trouble, so they walked out of the woods and onto the station platform, watching as the passengers came off the train.

Eventually, Boss saw his mother making her way off the steps of the train. She was dressed fashionably and was a lovely looking woman. But where was Rhoda?

Boss hugged his mother and then she hugged Henry Berry. It was good to be home. Boss quickly picked up his mother's bags, and they started to walk toward The Settlement. The woman laughed and seemed to beam with the reality of finally being home again, surrounded by family.

As they walked on, it occurred to Henry Berry that they were so preoccupied with Mrs. Strong, that Rhoda had been forgotten. He turned to look for her and for a moment didn't see her. Then it dawned on him that

there was a group of men all vying for a woman's attention. When the woman turned toward Henry Berry, he too was mesmerized by her beauty. Her long dark hair seemed to frame the beauty of her face like a work of art. This woman was gorgeous! This woman was Rhody?!

Henry Berry could feel the heat rise in his face and a squeeze of his heart. But, before he could move, Rhoda brushed off the men around her and walked over to him. She smiled, looked into his eyes, and his heart skipped a beat just before it melted. His head seemed to swirl momentarily; then his smile grew, and his blue eyes twinkled with excitement.

"Rhody!" he said, "Don't you look the grown woman?"

She took him by the arm, and they walked off, following Boss and Cee.

As the little group walked past the general store, Rhoda noticed a lovely lady's hat in the window and wanted to go inside for a better look. Boss needed to pick up some chewing tobacco and was headed there, anyway. Mrs. Strong, Cee, told the trio to do their shopping while she went down the street to the drug store. Henry was ready to follow Rhoda anywhere.

Inside the hardware store, Rhoda went directly to the window to have a closer look at that hat. She tried it on, but it was way too large for her, which made Henry Berry laugh, and embarrassed her. So she stomped on his toes and stomped out the door to follow her mother to the drug store.

Boss began to clap and tap his foot like they were at a hoedown as Henry jumped about on his good leg holding his bruised foot in his hands.

Henry wasn't sure what had just happened. But he was coming to grips with the thought that he just might be falling in love with his best friend's sister!

He punched Boss in the shoulder, and the two men just smiled.

"Wow!" Boss said, "Rhoda sure has blossomed." Then his attention focused on a new item in the store, the Henry Rifle that could hold fifteen cartridges in a single loading.

The shop clerk read the gun's slogan, aloud, "Load a Henry rifle on Sunday, and you can shoot all week!"

Boss became mesmerized holding the almost magical weapon, a real marvel of modern technology, forgetting the law would not allow him to own a gun.

Henry Berry just smiled while absentmindedly picking up a rubber ball from the store's main counter. He bounced the ball and heard the distant sound of a woman cursing up a storm! Rhoda?! He ran to the door as the ball bounced across the floor, unattended.

Across the way, he saw a big man sitting in a horse and buggy holding Rhoda by her left arm as she struggled to get free. The big man lifted her off the ground with his right arm and onto his carriage while he pulled up on the horse's reins with his left hand to keep the animal stationary. Rhoda cursed and tried to hit the man with her free hand. The big man just laughed and tried to get Rhoda to sit beside him.

Henry Berry was all feet and elbows as he ran down the street to help Rhoda. As he reached the driver's side of the carriage, he leaped into the air to throttle this ruffian and ne'er do well.

While still in mid-leap, Henry Berry came to an abrupt halt, his arms and legs gyrating wildly in the air. The big man in the carriage had caught Henry Berry by the throat with his left hand and held him so his feet couldn't touch the ground.

The big man pulled Henry Berry close and spit curses into his face. Henry could smell the booze on the drunkard's breath, which was rancid and foul - almost enough to knock him unconscious.

As Henry Berry started to feel like someone was lowering a dark grey hood over his head, he realized he was looking into the face of a beast. A brute of a man with a high browed ridge above his eyes, receding hairline, small mean eyes, and swollen jowls framing a grim scowl about his thin lips.

The moment seemed to be fading along with his life when Henry Berry recognized this big man was Brantley Harris, Captain of the Home Guard.

"Hey! Ain't you a Lowrie?" Captain Harris wondered aloud, "' Cause I kill Lowries for free!"

Rhoda could see Henry Berry's blue eyes begin to fade to a dark grey and she understood the big man was going to choke Henry to death. With her free right hand, she picked the buggy whip out of its perch and swung it with all her might across the horse's hindquarters, which immediately got the horses attention and put it into motion.

The horse reared up and jolted the buggy forward. Harris dropped Henry Berry and Rhoda as he desperately tried to find the reins and gain control of the vehicle as the horse ran wild down the road.

Henry hit the ground like a sack of potatoes.

Rhoda had tumbled over the back of the buggy seat, bounced over the rear deck, did a three-sixty off the back and landed with a thud on her butt, in an upright posture on the ground with her dress over her head, momentarily stunned.

She pulled her dress down, and as her vision cleared, she could see Henry Berry lying in a heap a few feet away. She scrambled over to him and lifted his head and shoulders onto her lap.

Henry Berry felt light come again into his eyes, and as he drifted out of his dream-state, he saw an angel smiling down at him.

"Rhoda?" he gasped, "Are you....?" But he couldn't get all the words out. His throat felt like it was coated in broken glass.

Rhoda helped him to his feet and looked into his eyes to be sure he was not seriously hurt.

From a distance, they could still hear the curses of Captain Harris as his threats to kill all the Lowries faded down the lane.

As Henry Berry's eyes became more focused and inquisitive, Rhoda gave him a hug and said, "Bear! You're my hero! You saved my life!" Then she kissed him on the cheek.

Henry's smile seemed to wrap around his head as his eyes became so blue they sparkled with joy!

"Anytime," he said and walked off toward his home, not realizing his feet were actually touching the ground.

Boss and Mrs. Strong didn't see the assaults, just Henry walking jauntily away and Rhoda standing alone in the middle of the road looking tousled but smiling. They ran over to Rhoda and looked her over to ensure she was not hurt.

Rhoda was not hurt, but she looked a mess. Her hair was all mussed up. Her dress had a rip across the shoulder, and her elbow had a bad scrape. But her eyes beamed and her smile seemed to glow from within.

"He kissed me!" was all she could say. Her smile prevented her from saying anything more. All she could hear was her own heart beating excitedly.

As the three family members walked toward their home, Boss looked his rumpled sister over one more time and added, "That must have been some kiss!"

CHAPTER 2

Mrs. Norment loved taking the train to Argyle Plantation from her home in Rowland. It even seemed like the Alma & Little Rock Railroad was her own private railroad. After all, it did include a nicely outfitted private passenger car.

The railroad had been built to transport cotton, tobacco, corn, potatoes, and rice, as well as cattle and pigs from the southern part of the state up to Alma Station at Argyle. From there, the goods would be moved to boxcars on the W.R.C. Railroad to make the one-hundred-mile trip east to the Port of Wilmington, North Carolina.

On dark stormy nights, fast blockade-running ships of the Confederacy would run through the Union blockade and on to Bermuda where the cargo would be sold and shipped to England or France. This had been the South's only remaining lifeline to bring in much-needed supplies that would flow north to Raleigh, Petersburg, and Richmond.

But all that was passed now. With the fall of Wilmington, the Yankees controlled all the Confederate ports. They had a stranglehold on Old Dixie. Damn them all!

Mary Norment sat beside her husband, Major O. C. Norment, C.S.A., as they rode their train north the fifteen-mile distance between their plantation's depot and the depot at Argyle Plantation. They were on their way to Argyle because Mary's husband had a scheduled meeting with the officers of the Home Guard. For Mary, it was a chance to visit her best friend, Elizabeth McRae, at her lovely home at Argyle. It would be good for the women to catch up on all the news and, hopefully, something said would be funny enough to make them laugh. They were such girls when they were together.

The Norments, like the McRaes, were generous supporters of the war effort and the right to keep North Carolina a Free State (meaning a Slave State) and member of the Confederate States of America, where slavery would remain legal. That was, of course, if the Confederacy could win the war and keep the damn Yankees and their Federal government from telling the Confederacy and North Carolina what they could and could not do. It was all about States' Rights, or at least that's how they felt since they lost control over the Federal Government to that God damned commoner, Lincoln!

The entire trip Mary could not stop talking while Major Norment, who'd been married to his wife for thirty years, absentmindedly nodded and mumbled, "Ah huh," and just let his wife vent. After all, he wasn't listening to a thing the woman had to say. He was only aware of how events seemed to be turning, one last time, to let down the noble cause they had risked so much for.

Trees and open farmland whisked passed the train windows. Major Norment's thoughts kept going back to what he'd personally heard General Robert E. Lee say the only time the Major had the pleasure of meeting the man.

Lee had forewarned that with the siege of Richmond, should the Port of Wilmington fall to Union Forces, there would be no way to resupply and rearm his army and the war would be lost.

He could not hold out longer than three months with the supplies he had stored in Richmond.

Fort Fisher and the Port of Wilmington had fallen to the Yankees. Yet, he dared not mention this to his wife, who was depressed enough with the news of more of her friends becoming war widows. When would it stop? Too soon, it seemed, and not in favor of their beloved Southern Confederacy.

The little train's whistle blasted, signaling the folks at Alma that the train was about to arrive.

Mrs. Norment always sat on the left side of the train so she could look out the window and admire their approach to the grand manor home, Argyle, which was located about a half mile before the railroad stop.

Mary always got a thrill when visiting the spacious white Victorian home. The porch curved entirely around the house and allowed a person to sit and rock on whichever side of the house provided the most shade and perhaps the comfort of a cool breeze on a summer's day. It was a perfect vantage point for keeping an eye on the slaves working the estate's grounds and fields. It was an impressive, lovely home, and Mary could almost smell the freshly baked pies she knew Edith would have ready for the guests to enjoy.

As the train rounded the last curve and the land around Argyle came into view, Mary became quiet at the sight of so many Confederate Army tents set up in an orderly manner surrounding Argyle. The site was an abrupt reminder of the war and what it cost the citizens of the South. The war was not supposed to have lasted this long. So many were not supposed to die.

At the sight of the Grand Manor, Mary regained her voice and started talking again. This time at the rate of a mile a minute! The Major just smiled and tried to ignore her.

Ben, Elizabeth's manservant, was waiting with a horse and buggy to whisk them to the manor house of Argyle. Although the day was sunny, a winter chill was in the air, and everyone turned their collars up against the cold.

Soon they were at the front steps leading up to the porch that surrounded the impressive home.

Just before Major Norment could knock on the door, both front doors swung open framing Elizabeth in her crimson red gown, the one she'd worn only a few nights ago.

Standing there with her long dark hair flowing over her shoulders and a mischievous twinkle in her eyes, Elizabeth exclaimed, "Welcome, to Argyle! My dearest friends!"

Major Norment took it all in and got a twinkle in his eyes, too.

Mary was a little less impressed. "Elizabeth! Have you no shame? That's the dress you wore at the New Year's Eve party – not a week past."

Major Norment couldn't help himself and added: "I think you look great, and you can look that nice anytime you wish."

Elizabeth brushed them both off. "Don't be a fuddy-duddy. Where will I ever be able to wear this dress again? And I like it and can wear it any time I want." Then more mischief in her eyes as she dramatically announced, "Come in, my friends!" and, with a slight bow to the Major, "Hello Major."

The Major nodded and took off his hat as his reply. "How is the mother of the hero of the day defending the Port of Wilmington once again against the Yankee Warships?"

Elizabeth giggled. "That sure was long-winded and well-thought-out Owen. You thinking of going into politics? They both laughed at the thought. Then, Elizabeth added, "It is nice to know that Harlee is safe. And better still to know he's a hero, too!"

Then, as if she had forgotten her friend, she turned toward her, "Mary, you look so nice, today. Not as good as me," Elizabeth joked. "But a close second."

Mary and Elizabeth were old friends and more like sisters than close friends. They hugged each other sincerely, and both sighed heavily at the same time.

Elizabeth guided them, as any polite hostess would, to the library where her husband, the Colonel, and the

other officers were gathering. This, of course, was not necessary because the Norments were old and dear friends who had visited Argyle often, during better times. But etiquette called for such formalities; especially in the presence of the other Confederate officers of the Home Guard.

Before entering the library, Elizabeth knocked twice on the heavy door to announce the arrival of Major Norment, who saluted his commander, Colonel McRae. The Colonel and the other officers in the room returned his salute, none too crisp in their efforts.

Elizabeth then put her arm through Mary's, and they both smiled broadly for the gentlemen, which was easy because they were genuinely happy to be together once again. They excused themselves and told the men to enjoy their meeting and if they needed anything to just ring for one of the servants. The two women closed the library door behind them as the men listened to the women's banter fade away.

Finally, the Sergeant-at-Arms called the meeting to order, and everyone sat down around the room's heat source, a large brick fireplace in the center of the wall situated between ten-foot-high windows that allowed daylight to light up the room's interior. Colonel McRae remained standing with his back to the open fireplace where a fire crackled and popped.

"Men, as you know," stated the Colonel, "with the fall of Wilmington and with General Sherman's Army headed out of Savannah, it looks as though our days as a free country may be numbered. But, let me reiterate, we have not yet lost this war! With God's divine help, we may still snatch victory from defeat."

"But I must confide in you," said the Colonel in a stern voice, "and inform you of the latest news I've only just received from Richmond. Our Dear President Davis has decided, in these desperate hours, to recruit Richmond slaves and free-blacks to form a company of black

Confederate soldiers with the promise to make them free citizens if they will fight against our Yankee foe."

Every man in the room stood up at this incredulous news! They all began to protest, but the Colonel just held up his open hand and pressed on. "Everyone here and everyone in our great country has risked life and treasure to remain free and maintain our way of life, as well as our proper place in the community. We have all sacrificed much, and some of us have sacrificed everything," said the Colonel biting his lower lip.

He turned to face the fire and punched his open hand with his fist and took a very deep breath, and then sighed slowly before continuing. He turned back to face his officers.

"Gentlemen, I think we all agree that if our cause is in such dire straits that we must ask for assistance from our own chattel in order to continue our struggles, I think we have lost this war! Because, if we give the blacks guns and ask them to protect us, why did we leave the Union in the first place? Not so long ago, our political leaders were most confident that the North could not survive without our cotton and our riches. They decided war was better than remain part of the Union. Now, Lincoln and his cronies can do whatever they wish once the war ends.

"Should we lose this war, gentlemen, I should not have to remind you what happens to the officers of the losing side. I suggest you all get your estates in order.

"And, gentlemen," Colonel McRae continued, "Sherman has marched through Georgia leaving Atlanta burned to the ground, and his army has taken the Port of Savannah. We have conflicting reports about his armies' movements and whereabouts, but we think he will either march to Wilmington to reinforce the Union force there; or, he is marching to take Augusta. Again, I advise you all get your things in order, for we may have some bad days coming our way."

The men were stunned by the news. They just sat and stared at the fire, contemplating what it all meant. God had abandoned them and their country. Perhaps God was against slavery after all? Even England had abandoned slavery thirty years ago.

Colonel McRae could almost feel his men being drained of energy. The war had gone on much longer than anyone had anticipated. No one had thought the North could defeat the mighty Southern States and their just cause for freedom and self-rule.

A knock came at the library door, and a young soldier came in and stood at attention, saluted and stated he had a telegram for Colonel McRae. The soldier held out the telegram in his right hand.

Major Norment took the envelope and passed it on to Colonel McRae who read the telegram, folded it, and placed it in his pocket.

Quickly, the Colonel straightened his own shoulders and stood more erect. "Gentlemen, we are not finished, yet! If Richmond falls, Lee's army can still survive to fight another day, and we must inform him that we will do whatever is necessary to keep our armies supplied and fed. And we will find a way to do that! I want Major Townsend and Captain King to work on procuring the means to move whatever supplies we can gather up to Virginia so that Lee can continue the fight."

The room would remain silent for what seemed like an eternity as each man contemplated failure. Most of the officers tried to find answers within the flames, dancing along the logs in the fireplace.

The meeting was adjourned, and all the officers left the room except Colonel McRae and Major Norment. When the library doors closed once again, Colonel McRae took the paper out of his pocket and handed it to Major Norment without saying a word.

The Major unfolded the single sheet of paper and silently read the message:

TO COLONEL NEIL MCRAE

STOP

THIS IS TO INFORM YOU OF

THE DEATH OF YOUR SON

CAPTAIN HARLEE MCRAE

STOP

KILLED IN ACTION

FORT FISHER

JANUARY 14, 1865

STOP

CHAPTER 3

The dense swamps between Maxtown and Lumberton were a safe haven for the local Indian men, runaway slaves, rebel deserters, and Yankee prisoners who'd escaped from the Rebel prison just outside Florence, South Carolina.

For years, these swamps had been a major resting and staging area for runaway slaves as they made their way north along the rivers and streams to avoid the dogs because they can't track a person through the water. The safety of the region and the care and generosity of the local Indians helped many a black person move safely through this portion of what would become known as the *Underground Railroad*.

Since the war began, family and friends of the men hiding out in the swamps had provided them with food. Though, usually, all they were able to offer was a little rice, corn, or maybe sweet potatoes. But now that the war had raged on for four years and everything available had been shipped to the war effort, the families on their small farms had no more food for themselves and, therefore, nothing to feed the men in hiding.

The only solution for their people to survive was for the men to come out of the swamp, steal from the rich, and distribute what they'd taken among the people in their community. After all, if Robin Hood could rob the rich and give to the poor in Jolly Old England, they could do the same in North Carolina. Desperate times required desperate actions.

The ten men hiding out in the swamp at a long-forgotten lumber camp they nicknamed the *Devil's Den* made up the core group that became known as the Lowrie Gang.

In truth, they were a gang of brothers that included Rhoda's two brothers. Boss, the youngest of the Strong brothers, was still growing, yet he already had a barrel-chest and thick arms. His older brother, by ten years, was Andrew, who stood over six feet tall. He had a slim build, and his complexion was almost white. He had his father's reddish hair. He held such a deep-seated disdain for slave owners that it bordered on murderous contempt.

Another set of brothers were the Oxendines. Calvin and Henderson Oxendine both had black "Indian" hair and dark brown eyes. They looked so much alike that from a distance you couldn't tell the two brothers apart. They, like the Strongs, were cousins of the Lowries, on their mother's side of the family.

Then, there were the Lowrie brothers, William, Thomas, Steven and Henry Berry.

William was in his thirties when the gang first came together. He was an intelligent, levelheaded man and a natural leader. The other men in the group never questioned his leadership and they had looked to him for guidance, even before the war began.

Tom was of a darker hue than his brothers which caused some to say he had the look of a Gypsy. Someone with a sneaky nature, because he was always alert and could take in everything around him with a single glance.

Steven Lowrie was the oldest brother and oldest member of the gang at age thirty-six. He had straight black hair and eyes so dark they seemed black. And, although he wore a thin black mustache, it was said he looked the "most Indian" of them all. That was likely due to his insolent manner toward whites. He was the most feared of the gang because he had an imperious temper, especially when he was drunk.

In fact, one evening at the Devil's Den, when William was away, Steven and Andrew Strong got drunk and decided the gang should go on a killing spree. Their "little brother," Henry Berry, who was sitting across the table from Steven, cleaning and loading an old Navy Colt Revolver, stopped them by stating that the men

were to stay in the cabin and sleep off their plans. Steven was insulted that his little brother could jump to "second in command" on his own and let out a few choice words, becoming so enraged he pulled his knife and said he'd stick it in...

That was all Steven had time to say or do because Henry shot him just below his left eye!

As the black powder smoke hung about the room and everyone's ears rang, Steven thrashed about in pain and disbelief. "You shot me!" he screamed. "You shot your own brother?"

Calmly, Henry said, "I won't let you or anyone else risk the safety of our families. So, just shut up and wash your face."

Steven kept pawing at his left cheek and holding his hand in front of his good eye, looking for blood. He couldn't believe there was no blood. His face, his eye, his cheek burned with pain. Heck, he couldn't believe he was alive after being shot in the face!

"Steven, you're not shot. You're just damned lucky I fired the cylinder that I hadn't yet loaded."

Indeed, Henry had cleaned the gun, loaded powder and wad, even put a percussion cap on the gun's cylinder-nipple. He just didn't complete the loading process by crimping in a lead ball. Steven had been hit with the round's wad of cloth. No bullet was fired.

Immediately, Henry Berry cocked his pistol again when he thought he saw anger returning to his brother's face.

"Tom, make no mistake. This here round is chambered with a solid lead bullet, and I will kill you dead if you don't quit your meanness and start to calm down."

It was enough of a warning to Steven and the rest of the gang that Henry Berry had become a man who would not be intimated or threatened. After this one demonstration of his leadership skills and cold, calculating disposition, no one ever questioned his orders again.

The only non-family members of the gang at this time were George Applewhite, a thin, wiry black man, and ex-slave-on-the-run, who could be counted on in a fight to protect your back. The youngest of the gang was a poor white boy with no family of his own, Zach T. McLauchlin.

If you asked a white person, they'd likely tell you the Lowrie gang was made up of between fifty and two hundred hardened thugs. There was no way they would believe the band was only a small group of brothers, cousins, and friends who were trying to survive desperate times and who, most of all, wanted to help their families.

The men broke up into two squads of five men each. Each group selected a different area of the region to search for white homes from which they could steal food and clothing. At first, they tried to locate isolated households where the man of the house was either a soldier away or dead, leaving the home protected only by a lone woman.

All the white homeowners in the area soon began to view oncoming darkness as fraught with terror as they imagined Indians entering their home in the middle of the night.

None of the homeowners had tried to resist or interfere with the robbers, except for the squad Henry Berry was with, led by his older brother, William. After entering the house, Henry began walking up the stairs to the bedrooms on the second floor when a wild-eyed old woman dressed only in a nighty so thin that each shot from her double-barreled shotgun lit up the hallway so brightly that Henry could see the old woman's naked body beneath the nightgown. The shotgun pellets went above Henry's head and into the walls scaring the wits out of the young man as he and the rest of the gang beat a hasty retreat from the house with only some pots and pans for their effort.

Later, Henry Berry would admit that seeing that old white woman naked was scarier than being shot at!

Once the laughter died down, they all agreed that robbing the rich and giving to the poor was going to be a risky business. One that would surely bring the Sheriff and the Home Guard looking for them and these "community leaders" would shoot to kill. The gang needed to arm themselves so they could at least have a fighting chance against their white neighbors. So far that night, they'd stolen all the guns they could find. But, only one looked like it was safe to shoot and there was no ammunition for the weapon.

Little Zach McLauchlin spoke up and immediately got everyone's attention. That afternoon he had been in Lumberton and noticed that there were no guards at the Armory. It seemed every available soldier was ordered to evacuate and assemble near Charlotte to form up a force to repel, or at least slowdown, the advance of Sherman's Army while protecting the gold in the mint at Charlotte.

William and Henry Berry Lowrie, Henderson Oxendine and Zach McLauchlin made the trek to inspect the

Armory themselves. Sure enough, there were no guards at the old building. The men broke the lock on the back door, that was out of sight from the roadway and cautiously took a look inside the dark warehouse. From the ambient starlight, they could make out stacks of crates that almost filled the large room.

William reached into his vest pocket, pulled out a wooden match, and scratched it along an iron door latch, causing it to burst into flame. As the fire illuminated the room's interior, William got a quick glance at the white cloud of noxious smoke billowing up toward his nose, causing him to quickly sidestep the odiferous sulfuric gas rising from the ignition of the match head.

Once in clean air again, William stood straight and walked over to the closest stack of crates. He noticed the markings seemed to be the same on all the boxes, as far as he could tell from the match light's limited reach.

William quickly put the first match out and lit another, trying to make out the letters on the boxes. He called Henry Berry over to look at the lettering. "Ain't this box got your name on it?" asked William. He shook off the fire from the match, and the room went pitch black again as his eyes tried to adjust to the abrupt change from bright to dark.

Both William and Henry Berry were unschooled, and neither could read or write thanks to the laws passed by the white citizens who reasoned it was beyond the Indian's station and intellect. However, Henry had seen his name in print often enough to recognize it when he saw it.

Both men pulled knives from their sheaths and began to pry off the lid of the box in front of them. Several of the nails holding the top in place made horrible screeching sounds as they clawed to keep a grip in the wood. With the lid finally off, William lit a new match. Lo and behold! The box was full of brand-new Henry Repeating Rifles!

Henry Berry pulled the rifle nearest him out of the crate, held it to his shoulder to aim, and then worked the lever a couple times to watch the ejector move through its eject-reload cycle.

Both men stood for a moment as they stared at the weapon and the significance of their find bean to sink in. These guns were a wonder of technology to behold; a gun that they would never be able to afford, and yet, here they were surrounded by stacks of crates full of these rifles!

The light suddenly dimmed, and William yelped as he absentmindedly held the match too long. William used his hands to feel for another rifle inside the crate. When his hands came to rest on a gunstock, he lifted the gun out and felt righteous with its potential power.

"Let me know when your eyes adjust to the darkness because we need to see if there's any ammunition for these rifles," directed William from the blackness.

As their pupils dilated, both men could only make out vague outlines of crates and other obstacles before them. Like blind men, they slowly made their way down each side of the aisle, feeling for a change in the size of the stacked crates.

Finally, Henry said, "William, this feels like it's a different size box. You want me to light a match and take a look-see?"

"Hold on a second. Let me keep looking a bit before you light up." was William's reply.

A few moments later, William spoke, "Alright, light 'er up! I've come to different boxes here, too."

Henry Berry struck a match across the wooden crate's grain, and quickly a flame flared into life illuminating the area once again.

Quickly Henry pried off the top of the box before him and found it full of new Navy Revolvers. These were older models that required brass percussion caps to fire off a round. However, these pistols did have revolving chambers for six rounds, and the chambers could quickly be swapped out and exchanged for another preloaded chamber ready to continue firing. It was another pleasant surprise.

William lit a match of his own and quickly opened the box in front of him. "Good news! There seem to be boxes of ammunition for the Henry Rifles here, too."

Again, in the dark, William set the rifle he was holding down, so the gun was pointed upward. He felt around the end of the barrel until he found the loading tube. He then felt around the box in front of him until he had a handful of cartridges. In the darkness, by touch alone, he dropped each cartridge into the tube. Then,

momentarily holding his breath, he cocked the rifle and quickly repeated the action. Somewhere off to his right, unseen in the shadows, William heard the satisfying clatter of a metal cartridge bouncing off the floor.

Henry gave no reply, but William knew his brother's smile was as big as his own.

The walk back to the door they'd entered was more manageable because when they called their cousin's name, the man standing guard at the door opened it, allowing starlight to show them the way out.

When William appeared at the doorway, his cousin, Henderson Oxendine, stood back and ensured the door remained wide open.

Outside in the starlight, William handed rifles to the two men who had waited outside. As dark as the evening was, these men's big smiles could be seen from far away. Zach McLauchlin beamed as he held the new rifle in his hands. All he could say was, "Great!" Cousin Oxendine simply said, "Perfect!"

"Let's take a box of rifles and a box of cartridges with us back to the Devil's Den," William said, "Then we can get the others to wake up everyone they can find to help us clean this warehouse out tonight. There may be Yankee guards here tomorrow or Rebs. Either way, won't make much difference. We need to take this stuff tonight!"

As they made their way over to where they'd left the canoes, the men wondered aloud why the Armory wasn't guarded.

"Could be the Rebs heard Sherman's Army maybe is headed this way and they all just skedaddled before he comes up here," offered Zach.

"Or, maybe they left because the Yanks are moving westward after taking Wilmington," Henderson Oxendine suggested.

"Don't matter why," said Henry Berry. "What matters is we got to lay claim to what's in the warehouse tonight because it might be early tomorrow when someone

finds there are no guards here. And you can bet there won't be a lot of goodwill to go round when they find all their stuff gone."

By midnight, the men had returned with forty of their family and friends. By 4:00 a.m., the Armory was empty. As a show of respect for civic duty, they made sure the doors were locked before they departed. During times such as these, folks couldn't be too careful.

CHAPTER 4

Elizabeth had not left her bedroom in over a week. She was exhausted from mourning the loss of her only child. Her grief filled her with depression. Nothing was the way it was supposed to be.

She'd try, on occasion, to sit up in bed. But reality made her so dizzy she thought she might throw up. She continued to lay in bed, hoping she could sleep and dream of better times.

Her best friend, Mary Norment, had not left her side since the news of Harlee's death. Both women were exhausted. Mary sat in a chair beside the bed and held Elizabeth's hand. Though neither woman spoke, Mary could feel Elizabeth's hand tremble with grief. Even with her eyes closed, as though she was sleeping, tears would roll down Elizabeth's cheeks, and her chest would heave. Mary wondered if her friend might die from grief.

Downstairs, cigar smoke cloaked the library and mixed with smoke from oak cordwood burning in the big brick fireplace. Colonel McRae had called all the officers of the Home Guard to meet that morning, and they all arrived on time, as expected. The news the colonel needed to convey to his commanders was such that immediate steps needed be taken to have any chance of winning this damned war.

"Men, Sherman's Army has been reported to be moving toward Columbia, South Carolina. This means the Yankees are only days away. We'll need to prepare as much resistance as we can muster if we are to slow Sherman's march north. No doubt, his goal is to link up his army with Grant's in Petersburg and together they'll take Richmond.

"We must try to give Lee and his Army of Virginia a chance to slip out of Richmond and regroup to fight another day. We may win this war, yet!" stated the Colonel as he hammered his fist on the tabletop. He then turned around to face the fire to warm his chest and cool off his hindquarters. He took a long drag on his cigar and exhaled a thick puff of smoke toward the jumping flames in the fireplace. He also wanted to allow what he'd just said to sink in for a moment, to let his officers contemplate the gravity of the situation. He rubbed his hands together closer to the fireplace and then turned back to face his men surrounding the table in front of him.

"Also, I'm getting reports of desertions—two and three men a day. Is there any way we can put a stop to this? Any suggestions?" implored the colonel.

No one, in particular, wished to reply so they all just sort of mumbled together apparent reasons for men quitting the fight and going home.

"They feel the war is lost and they need to go home to be with and protect their wives, family, and property," offered one officer.

"They don't want to be the last soldier killed when the war is ended," another officer was heard to say.

"They're frustrated, fed up, hungry, tired, sore and sick," continued someone from the room's corner.

"Enough!" said the colonel in a loud, deep, commanding voice. He held up his hand. "I don't want to hear any more. The fault is mine, gentlemen. I was thinking out loud. It was a foolish rhetorical question. Do what you can to keep our units together and functioning as part of the war effort. Can you do this?"

The officers just nodded their heads, less than enthusiastic in their lie.

"Captain Harris!" barked the colonel.

"Yes, sir?" snapped the captain.

"I've received reports of weapons stolen from the Armory in Lumberton. What information do you have pertaining to this incident?"

The captain took just a little too long to answer, making the air in the room seem dense and the walls seem to close in on everyone. Finally, the captain spoke up just before the colonel lost his temper.

"Colonel, I'm not certain if the last shipment of weapons made it into the warehouse. I mean, the Armory," blurted the captain as he tried to sound convincing. "It may be the shipment was captured by the Yankees spreading out from Wilmington. Or, more than likely, it's the damned local Indians. You know, that Lowrie Gang. They likely stole the items to sell for cash to Sherman's Army or to give to niggers and slaves to wage war against us. That's my guess," stated the captain, quickly adding, "Sir!" for he knew the colonel was in no mood for insubordination.

"Okay, captain, this is what I want you to do," ordered the colonel. "I want you to take fifteen or so men, and I want you to get to the bottom of this. Do you understand?"

"Yes, Sir!" replied the captain. "I can do that."

The captain just stood and stared for a moment.

"NOW, Captain!" shouted the colonel.

The rage in the colonel's orders caused the big man to push back and scoot the chair away from the main table. But, one of the chair legs caught on an uneven floorboard and the leg broke, sending the fat man tumbling over backward across the floor.

The colonel turned back toward the fireplace and listened as the fat man struggled to get up off the floor with the assistance of the other officers. The colonel stared into the flames absentmindedly and rubbed both sides of his head, trying to massage away the tension and frustration.

Late that afternoon, the captain and his assembled squad appeared on the lane leading up to the house of Allen Lowrie, father of the Lowrie boys. As the men of the Home Guard approached the house, Allen's wife, Pollie, walked out of the house and onto the front porch to meet the trespassers.

"What do you want?" asked Pollie, the vehemence apparent in her voice.

"Where's your husband, Allen, and your sons?" shouted the captain.

From the porch, Pollie could see her husband and son toiling in the field a few hundred yards away. The Home Guard had not seen the men because a patch of trees separated the fields from the roadway and, like most whites; the men focused entirely on what was in front of them, and not their surroundings. Pollie understood that even if she lied to the captain, as soon as he and his squad turned around to leave, they would have a clear view of her husband and son in the field. She paused, trying to buy time, trying not to look in the direction of her family members, trying to see by way of her peripheral vision if her men saw the intruders and would take flight into the woods. Alas, the men were working their way down the furrow of the field and had their backs toward the house. They were not aware of the danger.

Before the captain could become frustrated and angry, Pollie lifted her right arm and pointed toward the open field.

"There they is, talk with them and then get the hell off our property," Pollie declared.

"Don't you act uppity to us woman or you'll be sorry. You hear?" growled the fat man sitting in his horse and buggy with his men standing behind the vehicle in military formation. He needed to demand respect from this woman if he was to expect it from his own men.

"Corporal!" shouted the fat captain as he waved his arm to signal the man to appear beside him, so he didn't have to try to look over his shoulder at the man.

"Yes, sir?" asked the corporal.

"Corporal, I want you to take three men and escort this woman and her children over to that shed there. I want you to tie them up and place a guard to hold them there until I'm finished here. Is that understood?" directed the captain.

"Yes, sir!" said the corporal, who saluted the captain and went back to select the men to follow him and carry out the captain's orders.

"And corporal" added the captain.

"Yes, sir?"

"Search the house, barn, and anywhere they may be hiding stolen property. Especially be on the lookout for any guns you can find," barked the big man.

"Yes, sir, right away, sir!" said the corporal with a quick salute. He led his men through the house, rounding up and arresting Pollie, her two young boys and baby daughter and guided them to the storage shed behind the main house. The Lowries were tied up, left in the shed, the door locked and a guard was posted outside.

CHAPTER 5

Henry Berry had been spending the day at the Strongs' house with his best friend, Boss, and to be near his little friend now all grown up, the lovely and desirable Rhoda. He was about to leave and head home when one of the neighbor's boys came running up and told them that their young cousin, Jarman Lowrie, had been shot dead!

"Who? How?" were the first words out of Henry's mouth as his mind raced. He felt like he was going into shock.

The boy had to take a minute to catch his breath, as he'd just run a distance of almost four miles. After a moment and a drink of water, the boy was calm enough to blurt out that Brantley Harris had been drunk and driving down the road when he saw an Indian boy cross the road ahead of him. When he got up to the footpath the boy had taken, he could see Jarman standing facing an old oak tree taking a piss.

Harris thought he recognized the boy and yelled out, "Lowrie, is that you?"

Jarman hollered back over his shoulder, "Yep, it's me."

Harris picked up his shotgun and shot Jarman in the back!

"We found Jarman a while ago and just before he died, he said he'd turned to take a look-see at who'd shot him. That's when Harris said, 'Ah shit, wrong Lowrie. Sorry, boy, I thought you was Henry Berry', and then Harris just rode on off with not a care in the world."

"Of course he ain't got no care in the world. He knows Indians can't testify against a white man. Besides, who we going to for help? The sheriff ain't going to arrest Captain Brantley Harris of the Home Guard," said

Henry Berry. He was right, too. Didn't no one who was white care what happened to an Indian unless it meant they could take the Indian's land.

Rhoda fell into Henry's arms and cried her heart out for the loss of their friend and relative. It seemed there was always another funeral to attend. When was it all going to stop?

Boss finally came over and pulled his sister from his friend's arms. Everyone was crying about the news. It hurt. It hurt deep. Jarman was still a kid with a long life ahead of him and he had never done no harm to no one. Now, he was dead just because some fat slob of an asshole thought it a fun sport to shoot Indians.

"Where was Jesus? How many times can a man turn his cheek?" cried Rhoda as she allowed Boss to take her into their home.

Henry Berry headed home before the afternoon sun was too low over the trees. The shadows of the trees seemed as though they were ghosts of friends and family killed by these bigots and slave owners. What made them think they were so much better than other people that they could literally get away with murder? Who gave them that right? Why did God allow this?

Too many questions weighed heavily on young Henry Berry and there was no urgency in the heavy steps he took today knowing when he arrived home, he'd have to tell his mom and she'd surely fall into a fit of grief.

As usual, he took a shortcut home through the woods following old game trails and personal hidden paths that he and his brothers and friends had established over a lifetime of exploring.

Soon, he came to the edge of the forest behind his family's house. Immediately he dropped down to one knee when he saw the Home Guard moving through the buildings and taking his rope-bound mother and siblings into the storage shed, locking the door behind them, a guard posted at the door.

Staying low, he quietly moved to the other side of the house so he could look out over the freshly turned fields where he could see a group of the Home Guard marching behind two men riding in a horse and buggy. Henry didn't recognize the passenger. But the driver, Henry, knew well. "Harris!" Henry hissed softly through clenched teeth.

Henry then realized the group was moving over the field to where two men were standing, watching the Home Guard approach. The man leaning against his hoe was his dad, Allen. The other man was his brother, William. Both men just stood and watched, and waited for the men of the Home Guard to come to them. This was their safest tactic. This late in the war, with Fort Fisher having fallen to the Yankees, there wasn't much need for slave labor. To try to run away at this point would likely only get one or both men shot in the back.

As the group of men talked, one of the men who'd been looking through their possessions came up to Captain Harris's buggy and handed him a rifle. Harris took the weapon and then pointed his finger accusingly at Allen and William, who shook their heads from side to side indicating they knew nothing of the rifle.

Harris made a grand gesture to his men, and they surrounded Allen and William, tying their hands behind their backs and guiding them to sit on the back of the buggy. The group then rode away from the road and further back into the property, toward the river.

"Why are they going toward the river?" Henry wondered to himself. "The town and the Sheriff's Office are in the other direction."

Henry decided to follow the group. But, he had to be careful not to be seen or he'd end up surrounded by Home Guardsmen, too.

Henry quickly ducked back into the deepening shadows of the thick forest vegetation. Almost immediately, he found one of the hidden paths used to skirt the open fields. He had to run swiftly, though, because he had to run *around* the cleared fields, staying hidden in the woods while trying to keep the group in sight.

Eventually, he lost sight of the group because he had to go deeper into the woods to avoid swimming across a pond, which would not only take more time but would expose his position. By the time he caught up to where the Home Guard had stopped, he could see his brother and father were tied up and blindfolded in front of the lined-up Home Guardsmen.

But why? This couldn't be about the Armory heist, because the rifles they'd stolen were Henry Repeaters. The rifle handed to Harris looked to be an old single shot Springfield even from the distance where he sat.

The passenger in the buggy, obviously the officer-in-charge, said something and motioned to Harris, who saluted and returned to the line of armed men facing his father and brother. The group was too far away from Henry Berry for him to hear what was being said.

Henry could clearly see the officer in the buggy. The image of the man's face would, in the future, cause him to wake from a sound sleep, sweating with his heart pounding. Who *was* this man?

Harris walked over to where the men had gathered in front of Henry Berry's bound and blindfolded kinfolk. A command was shouted, and the line of men snapped to attention. A second later, the sound of Harris's voice traveled to where Henry lay. "READY!" Henry saw

Harris once again shout, and the line of men snapped their rifles up against their shoulders. A second later, the command was heard, "AIM!", and the guns were pointed at his father and brother.

Then a final shout followed by daggers of fire and bellows of smoke emitting from each rifle. Great globs of blood and tissue erupted behind both the men's heads and bodies standing in front of those murderous rifles. The men seemed to stand defiantly for what seemed, to Henry, to be ages. He gasped at the sight. His heart seemed to stop. He couldn't breathe, and that old gray curtain seemed to lower itself over his eyes.

A second later, Henry faintly heard the word "FIRE!" Followed immediately by a loud *BOOM* as the full concussion from the exploding shots reached his ears. He was also aware that the discharge had jolted him and made him jump. Had he been hit, too?

When he drew his next breath, he thought he was dead because, as he opened his eyes, he couldn't see anything! All was dark around him. He was alone and confused and laying in the woods. His head hurt. His chest hurt. But, as he slowly checked himself over, he could not find any wounds.

What had happened? Why? Where was he? What day and time was it? His head was spinning, and he was going to pass out again. So, he lay back onto the soft moss where he'd found himself and allowed the spinning in his head to stop on its own.

He started to think back through the events of the afternoon, and then it all crashed again upon him. He knew where he was and what he'd seen. He jumped up, burst out of the tree line, and ran across the field to where he'd seen his brother and father fall. But their bodies weren't there. Maybe he was dreaming?

The clouds in the night sky parted just long enough to allow moonlight to illuminate the bloody pools where the men had fallen. Henry knelt down and touched the spots with his fingers, then held them up close to his face to catch as much moonlight as possible until he could see the blood on his hands.

Confused, and still in shock, he wandered down the dirt road to report the deaths... to who?

He moved forward in a dazed state and stumbled along the road.

Eventually, he sat on a fallen log beside the road and just stared at his hands. His mind and senses were overloaded, and all he could do was stare mindlessly at the blood on his hands.

Henry first became aware of the dawn's light when he realized a horse and wagon had come slowly walking around the curve in the road before him. As the carriage completed the turn, the driver spotted a man, sitting on a fallen tree. The carriage driver pulled up on the reins and brought the horse and vehicle to a stop in front of the man sitting with his head bowed.

Henry looked up and stared at what, at first, appeared to be the apparition of Death. Strangely, Death seemed to be a fat man. The carriage driver was Captain Brantley Harris, heading home after being drunk all night with one of the women he controlled and abused. He started to say something derogative to the Indian but stopped short as he noticed something wasn't right about the way the Indian looked at him.

No matter. "Well God Damn! If'n it ain't THE Henry Berry in the flesh! This time I'm gonna kill you dead, son," said Captain Harris.

Too bad the light was so low at that time of the morning because if Harris had seen Henry's eyes in the light of day, he would have taken note that those ordinarily twinkling mischievous blue eyes were now a void of blackness that foretold of a calm, cold and deadly disposition. Henry Berry was a predator coiled to attack.

As Harris pulled his shotgun from the back of the buggy, he cocked one barrel and began to take aim at Henry.

Henry Berry wasn't even aware of his own movements. He was up and with two steps he bounded off the log he'd been sitting on and launched himself at Captain Harris. Henry drove himself into the big man's chest, his shoulder stopped the shotgun from lowering further, and the gun fired harmlessly into the air. The force of Henry's tackle sent both men over the back of the carriage seat landing Harris on the back deck and Henry Berry lying in the dirt behind the vehicle.

As Harris reached behind his back for his waist pistol, Henry Berry's perception of time moved in slow motion as he picked up the shotgun that had fallen on the ground beside him, cocked both hammers and pulled both triggers. A blink of an eye later, fire spits out from one of the barrels. Instantaneously, Harris yelped as lead pellets tore through his heart, out his back, and showered blood onto the horse's back. Between the deafening blast and the feel of wet blood and tissue assaulting the nag's hindquarters, the startled animal reared up and took off down the lane like a bat out of hell. Around the corner, the carriage went, and just as suddenly as it had appeared, it was gone.

Henry Berry found himself alone, sitting in the road not entirely understanding what had just happened.

He was aware, though, of some good news. He'd just become the owner of a double-barrel shotgun.

CHAPTER 6

Even if the Indians had access to the local newspapers, it wouldn't have mattered because they couldn't read. The articles and advertisements were *for the citizens by the citizens,* because the wealthy whites who paid to keep the news flowing saw to it that the stories told the "truth" as long as they followed the accepted rules and presented their stories with a white person's slant.

This is the actual story from the *Lumberton Robesonian* newspaper:

Maxtown, N.C. March 4, 1865 It is a misnomer to call the war in Robeson County by any other name than the war of the Bushmen, or The Lowrie War. It was waged in a spirit of revenge. They wish to retaliate on the white race because the Home Guard of the county found Allen Lowrie, their father; and William Lowrie, their brother, receivers of stolen goods from various parts of the surrounding country in the month of February 1865, and having court-martialed them and found them guilty, sentenced them to be shot. There is but one opinion in regard to this whole matter among the law-abiding citizens of Robeson County, and that is that Allen Lowrie, the old man, as he is termed, should have acted better toward his white neighbors, who had often befriended him, than to have received into his house stolen goods, taken from his neighbors, and then found to endeavor to screen himself and his son William from punishment. The verdict of the public is that he was 'particeps criminis,' equally guilty with his son William and that the Home Guard did right in passing sentence of death on them both and in carrying that sentence into execution. And right here is a moral lesson: 'The way of the transgressor is hard.' 'Vengeance is mine, and I will repay, saith the Lord,' 'The wicked live out half their days.' Behold! see! Henry Berry Lowrie and his associates in crime have gone to the criminals bourne, "to answer for the deeds done in the flesh,' and may their like never again appear on this world's arena, for they were the very cowards, the most arrant poltroons, that ever disgraced the annals of warfare." [1]

# # #

Few readers gave much thought to the killing of the Indians because the important news of the day was stated in the headline:

SHERMAN'S ARMY BURNS COLUMBIA!

The war was coming to their towns and there was much to be done, most of it in a near state of terror.

Most everyone found panic to be a great motivator.

Home Guard soldiers were either deserting or grouping together in their efforts to stop Sherman on his way to Charlotte and the city's gold reserves. Trenches were dug and families were evacuated westward. The bridges leading into the city were burned. The Home Guard might not be able to stop Sherman's Army but, by God, they could hold him at the river's edge.

Much to their chagrin, Sherman enlisted the aid of the local Indians to guide his army through the swamp, almost exactly between Charlotte and Wilmington. The Indians not only knew the waterways and the lay of the

---

[1] *The Lowrie History*, by Mary C. Norment

land but for years they'd been moving runaway slaves along the very same

route to freedom.

With the Indians guiding them, Sherman's Army went through North Carolina so quickly that even General Robert E. Lee's Army of Virginia would not be able to keep the combined armies of Grant and Sherman out of Richmond. In fact, it was Henderson Oxendine who led Sherman's scouts through the swamp, showing them the best route for Sherman's Army.

The Union Army dispatched swarms of soldiers into the countryside foraging for food and, most importantly, wooden rails. More than 25,000 rails were taken from disassembled split-rail fences surrounding the local farms. These split rails were used by Sherman's Core of Engineers to lay down a plank road over which the wagons and men could travel across the swamp. The troops referred to this plank road as a *corduroy road* because they thought the wagon wheels moving over the planks reminded them of the sound corduroy pants make when you're walking.

Henderson was glad to help get this war over as quickly as possible. When he returned to his farm, however, he discovered that Sherman's men had swept over his farm, too, and taken his only mule! "How is a person supposed to farm without a mule? *God damn it.*"

In Richmond, it was only the bravery and tenacity of General Lee and "his boys" that had kept the Union Armies at bay for 262 days. Now it looked like the end of the war would come soon enough.

When the Home Guard became aware that Sherman wasn't going to be stopped at Charlotte, but had, in fact, run through the swamps in the center of the state, they understood the only way a white man could find his way through the dense treacherous swamps was with the aid of the Indians as their guides.

Once they were assured Sherman was on his way to Richmond, the Home Guard devised a plan for payback against the Indians.

The soldiers who had accompanied Captain Harris when he arrested and executed Allen Lowrie returned to Pollie Lowrie's house and arrested her; and like her husband, she sat on the back deck of a wagon and was led away across the fields with her hands tied behind her back.

Once the small parade of Guardsmen reached the area where dried blood could still be seen, the drunken soldiers took off Pollie's blindfold so she could see the spot where she was to stand and the dried blood. She would know where she was and what had occurred.

The old woman was so lightheaded that the soldiers had to tie her to a nearby tree to keep her standing upright.

The Corporal leading the mob of armed men spat questions into Pollie's face.

"Where were the stolen guns hidden?

"Where did her traitorous sons hide out in the swamps?

"Who were the ones that led Sherman and his army through the swamps?"

To all questions, Pollie could only answer, truthfully, that she did not know.

Angrily, the Corporal replaced the blindfold over Pollie's eyes and stepped back to where his unit was standing in line before the woman.

Pollie listened as the Corporal shouted the words, "Ready, aim... Fire!"

In that instant, Pollie went out like a snuffed candle. Her world stopped and everything she'd known went black.

CHAPTER 7

When Henry Berry walked into his parent's house, he found the entire family crammed into the home's main room. The house was quiet except for the occasional whisper. No one knew what to do next.

Pollie continued to sit and stare into the fire in the hearth. She had not said a word to anyone since they'd found her blindfolded, unconscious and tied to a tree.

Henry's eyes frowned, and his jaw clenched as his brothers told him what they suspected had happened. If anyone had thought to look directly into Henry Berry's eyes, they would have seen a change and not just that his bright blue eyes had become dark black voids, but that those eyes foretold of a gathering storm that was about to be unleashed upon their tormentors.

Without saying a word, Henry Berry walked out of the house and headed back toward the Devil's Den.

He swore to take revenge on those involved with the death and misery inflicted on their people. From that point on, he'd kill any man who dared threaten the well-being of any of his family or friends.

CHAPTER 8

The War was over. The Southern States would be annexed to the United States of America and be forced into a country and way of life not wanted by the Southern Conservative Elite. Gone would be their part of the world where they lived like kings. Gone was their power to belittle and punish those who they felt did not do their share, as ordered. Gone were the days when they got respect and could go their own way.

Although Elizabeth had known for some time that the Yankees were winning the war, the news that General Robert E. Lee had surrendered to General Grant was a shock: too much bad news in too short a time. It seemed like only yesterday, her husband had informed her of their son's death. Harlee's death caused her to cry and mourn for two days and nights until she finally fell asleep from exhaustion. But now, with the news that war was lost, she just couldn't cry anymore. How many times had she cried at the news of another friend's loss of a son or husband because of the damned war?

Like a tune, she couldn't shake from her head, she kept trying to find the answer to one question, "Were all their tears worth it?"

The answer, of course, was "no," but she was too dumbfounded, too numb to realize it. The surviving rebels who fought for their cause and lost were given their lives by the victors, the Union.

However, the former rebels were forced to pledge allegiance to the United States of America and to never take up arms in rebellion again. This was all the Yankee's required of them as a condition of their parole?

Martial law was declared, and the Yankees sent in their troops to remake the South and free the slaves.

Were the Yankees preparing to make the whites subservient to their former chattel, their servants, the blacks? Hell, the blacks needed to be taken care of because they did not have the mental capacity to read, write, or even live by themselves, for the most part. Who was going to take care of them?

"Well, the Yankees can just take care of them!" blurted Elizabeth out loud to no one, surprising herself at the sound of her own voice.

Elizabeth felt herself shudder with the thought that the Yankees might come and burn Argyle Manor to the ground. Or, divide their land among the blacks. Well, she still had her loving husband, and he had made arrangements should the worst happen. He'd set up accounts in the Bermuda Islands, as well as accounts in England where the family had established business offices. They could leave this God forsaken country if need be.

At least, in the morning when she looked out over their land, she no longer had to look at the rows of army tents. The Home Guardsman had all packed up their gear and gone home to wherever home was.

A loud continuous knocking on the double front doors interrupted her sour mood.

Edith shouted, "I'm coming!" several times as she hobbled from the kitchen toward the front door.

When she opened the door, she was surprised to see Robert, a local white man that worked at the telegraph office over at the Argyle Depot. He was standing at the door, out of breath and white as a ghost.

"I got to see Colonel McRae right now!" stammered Robert, pushing his way into the foyer. "I got a telegram here that the Colonel needs to see! Where the hell is he, Edith?" the agitated man wanted to know.

"Why my goodness, Mr. Robert, what got into you?" The agitation in Robert's voice was uncharacteristic. "Massa McRae ain't back yet from his trip to Maxtown. Is there something I can do?" she asked.

Robert was jumping up and down with energy flowing through his veins when he noticed Elizabeth step from the parlor into the hallway. He nearly knocked Edith over in his exuberance to get past her and talk to Mrs. McRae.

Elizabeth didn't know what to make of the intrusion and was surprised when Robert pushed a telegram into her hand. He then started talking so fast, and so excitedly, it took her a moment to understand him. She held up her right hand with the palm of her hand, almost touching Robert's nose.

"You hush up now. Ya hear? Let me read the telegram," scolded Elizabeth.

Robert shut his mouth and waited silently in front of Elizabeth like a little boy waiting for his big surprise birthday present.

Elizabeth's lips moved as she silently read the telegram.

She stood motionless for a moment, trying to comprehend what she'd just read. Could it be true? Again, her lips moved silently, but more slowly this time as she carefully re-read each of the words so she could ensure she'd not misread the telegram.

A big grin swept over her lovely face, and twinkles appeared in her eyes. "Neal has to see this right away!" she shouted to Robert, who was standing only a foot or so in front of her. "You get back to the depot and forward this message to all points! Make sure the newspapers get this story out today!" she instructed

Robert as she pushed him out the front door. She immediately turned to run down the hallway and up the stairs to her bedroom. She wanted to fix herself up as pretty as could be so that her husband would be aroused by how beautiful she was and what a big difference a smile could make! He hadn't seen her smile in days, and he'd said so again in a very concerned voice just that very morning.

Edith tried without success to keep up with Elizabeth as she bounded up the stairs. Even with much effort, she fell further behind Elizabeth. Exasperated, she finally yelled up, "What on Earth do that paper say, Miss Betsy?"

"Lincoln has been shot dead by the rebel hero, John Wilkes Booth!" yelled Elizabeth over her shoulder as she jerked open dresser drawers and began pulling out lingerie to wear under her dress as a fun surprise for her husband. Despite all the recent bad news, it seemed a great deal of the weight had been lifted off her shoulders. This was the best news possible! Hell, the South just *might* rise again.

The next morning, Elizabeth was still asleep when her husband awoke. He was still smiling from the fantastic news and evening his wife had given him. He walked to the window and looked out at clear blue skies. Spring was in the air and he felt he could almost smell a new promising future.

The news spread quickly throughout the county and invitations sent to all the former officers of the regional Home Guard. The meeting was to be that night at Argyle Plantation. The men needed to coordinate their plans before the Yankee troops arrived to enforce martial law.

Colonel McRae ordered a new keg of Scotch to the manor house, for tonight was to be the start of a new beginning and would require many toasts to complement a new brotherhood.

Just after sunset, the officers of the old Home Guard began to arrive and gather in the library of Argyle Manor.

As usual, Major Norment and his wife were the last to arrive. Elizabeth escorted her friends into her home and announced their arrival in formal, yet friendly terms as they entered the library containing the other Home Guard Officers.

Elizabeth and Mary were so overjoyed to be together again that the moment was reason enough to giggle like schoolgirls. They left the men to their duties as their laughter and talking over each other blended with the magic of the night. Their voices faded away, and the door to the library closed behind them.

Colonel McRae stood in his usual spot before the grand fireplace, facing the men of his old unit. He stood silently before the men, patiently, as he waited for his manservant, Ben, to provide each officer with a full glass of Scotch. Once all the men had their goblets filled, and Ben had moved to his corner of the room to await further need, the Colonel raised his glass and made a toast.

"To all the men who can't be here tonight because they gave everything to the cause, which is our birthright. We give our thanks to God because he smote our persecutor and has shown us that with perseverance and cunning, the South will rise again! Amen!"

"Amen!" shouted the officers in response, and they all drank to complete the first toast of the night.

"Tonight, gentlemen, we are here to dissolve the North Carolina Unit of the Robeson County Home Guard of our beloved Confederate States of America. We are here tonight to renew our mission and, with the help of God, join a new cause and swear our allegiance to a new order. A new brotherhood of conservatives that will protect our land, women, families, and freedom from the heavy hands of those who wish to oppress us," sang Colonel McRae, sounding much like an Evangelical preacher.

"Amen, brother!" yelled someone in the group.

"Hallelujah to a new day for the South!" shouted another.

The Scotch was kicking in quickly tonight because this was the Colonel's "good stuff."

"Gentlemen," the Colonel continued, "I am here tonight to offer each of you the chance to join a fraternity and brotherhood to combat the lawlessness that has become rampant in our countryside. Membership in this fraternity will allow us to work with our powerful Conservative allies to undermine what is about to be unleashed upon us by those Yankee bastards that are preparing to bring martial law down upon our heads. I trust in my heart and soul that each of you feels as I do, that our cause is just and we must somehow keep the Northern invaders in check. Are you with me?" the Colonel shouted.

"Yes, Sir!" the group shouted in unison.

"Good! Then let's drink to a new commitment to each other and a new fraternal order!" the Colonel said triumphantly. Then, he and the other men lifted their glasses for another toast.

"Ben! Please see to it that everyone's glass is refilled and then you are free to join Edith in the kitchen," instructed the Colonel.

Ben did as he was told and ensured everyone's glass was refilled. A couple of the men grabbed his jacket sleeve to stop him before he moved on because they'd already kicked back the refill of Scotch and needed him to refill their goblets again.

Once satisfied everyone's glass was full, Ben turned and asked, "Colonel, will there be anything else I can do for you this evening?"

"No, thank you, Ben. I'll ring if we need you," said the Colonel and Ben left the room, closing the big doors behind him.

The Colonel listened as Ben's footsteps echoed down the hallway. When the sounds had faded sufficiently to make him feel they had complete privacy, the Colonel continued, "Men, I now turn the floor over to Major Norment, who will go through some formalities for induction into our new Fraternal Brotherhood.

"Major Norment, you now have the floor," said the Colonel as he walked toward an empty chair beside the fireplace.

The major stood and looked over the men present to gauge their mood. Satisfied he had their undivided attention, he began his prepared speech.

"Gentlemen, the Ku Klux is an institution of chivalry, humanity, mercy, and patriotism, embodying in its genius and its principles all that is chivalric in conduct, noble in sentiment, generous in manhood, and patriotic in purpose; its peculiar objects being: to protect the weak, the innocent, and the defenseless from the indignities, wrongs, and outrages of the lawless, the violent, and the brutal; to remember the injured and oppressed; to succor the suffering and unfortunate, especially the widows and orphans of Confederate soldiers; to protect and defend the Constitution of the

United States, and all laws passed to protect the states and the people thereof." [2]

At Major Norment's signal, the Sergeant at Arms standing next to the door of the room's entrance quickly opened the door and looked around the interior of the manor. Satisfied there was no one outside eavesdropping, the guard quietly closed door and nodded to the Major that all was clear.

"Fine," said the Major, "Then I'll ask you all to respond to the following questions to see if you are sincere enough in your commitments." Here, the Major paused again to gauge the group's response.

Reassured, the Major began reading aloud the questions for prospective members:

- "Do you believe in the superiority of the white race?

- "Do you promise never to marry any woman but one who belongs to the white race?

- "Will you, under all circumstances, defend and protect persons of the white race against all encroachments or invasions from any inferior race, especially the African?

- "Will you promise never to vote for anyone for an office of honor who does not belong to the white race?

- "Are you opposed to allowing the control of the political affairs of this country to go into the

---

[2] *The Annals of American*, Chapter 12, The Ku Klux Klan

> hands of the African race, and will you do everything in your power to prevent it?" 2

Every man in the group answered, "Yes!" to each question.

"Are you ready to swear the oath of allegiance to the Ku Klux Klan?" asked the Major, eagerly.

"Yes, sir!" the men answered with enthusiasm.

The Major straightened his posture, cleared his voice and then continued, "If you consent to join our Association, raise your right hand, and I will administer to you the oath. Repeat after me."

"I do solemnly swear, to maintain and defend the social and political superiority of the white race on this continent; always and in all places to observe a marked distinction between the white and African races; to vote for none but white men for any office of honor; and to devote my life and influence to instill these principles in the minds and hearts of others; and to defend all persons of the white race against the encroachments of the inferior black race.

I swear, moreover, to unite myself in heart, soul, and body with those who compose the Order; and to the faithful performance of this oath, I pledge my life and sacred honor. Amen." 3

"Amen," stated the men together.

"I will now instruct my new brothers as to the secret hand-sign, handshake, and password," intoned Major Norment, taking care to inform them about the particular circumstances and occasion of their use.

---

3 3 "*The Annals of America*" – 1868; the Encyclopedia Britannica Inc.

Once everyone in the room practiced the secret grips, signs, and handshakes, they all whispered the secret password to one another to ensure everyone was well versed in its use.

One final toast was proposed. *The South shall rise again!* And, the meeting adjourned.

CHAPTER 9

News of the war's end was met with a feeling of relief, a new hope for better days to come.

Even Pollie, the Lowrie matriarch, seemed to have become more alert and relaxed with the news. Although, when she looked into Henry Berry's eyes and saw the depth of the darkness, she could see his anger and intolerance for the oppression of his family and friends. Perhaps, somehow, the Indian men, instead of hiding, could protect their loved ones now that they had guns of their own? At least they might have a fighting chance instead of being tied up and shot.

Henry had nothing to say for several days and remained silent after he was told how family members had found their father and brother the day they were executed by the Home Guard. How they dug up the bodies of the men and brought them home where they were cleaned up and given a decent Christian burial. Evidently, Henry was still in his haze when the funeral was held because he wasn't seen for three days. His brothers had to perform the burial without his presence.

Henry's eyes had remained black, and the smile that had once seemed a permanent feature had disappeared. It was as though he'd aged twenty years in attitude and ten years physically. Overnight, the boy seemed to morph into a full-grown man; a man with little tolerance for those who made threats toward his family and friends.

Even with the war ended and soldiers staggering home exhausted, the dismal conditions seemed to linger for there was little to be found to eat on the small farms. This was especially true for the free blacks who included the Indians. Henry and his family and friends had to continue raiding the white farms and plantations where food, clothing, and blankets could be collected. The men would take everything of value they could find. The rich could always replace the items. The poor had no other way to obtain these necessary things.

Often, the gang would collect so many goods and so many items that they'd use the homeowner's own wagon and horse to move the ill-gotten gains into the swamp where they would unload their spoils. The horse and wagon would always be returned to its owner, who was thankful for small favors.

Working with the black and Indian churches throughout the area and The Settlement, the clothing, blankets and, primarily, the needed food, were distributed to those that needed it most, free of charge. The original Robin Hood would have been proud of their efforts.

Of course, this upset the white citizens of the county, so much so that they began a steady stream of complaints to the local sheriff and the state representatives. Henry Berry Lowrie and his gang were becoming well known to local law officials.

Even as the Indians held out hope for the future, news of incidents concerning friends and relatives would still come to light, and it was like pouring salt into open wounds.

Soon, there was word about two more of their close friends, William Locklear, and Hector Oxendine. The two were on their way to a white neighbor's house to inquire about their horses that had been confiscated by the Home Guard during the war when former members of the old Home Guard came upon them. They were immediately arrested by the whites, though after a brief discussion, they allowed William Locklear to leave unharmed. They kept Hector under arrest overnight because they believed he was one of the Indians who had led Sherman's Army through the swamps on their way to Richmond.

The next day, word was sent to another white neighbor, Andrew Carlisle, that he was needed to "help shoot a buck." Andrew was most interested in being a part of this because he blamed Hector for the loss of his own horses and all the split rail fences around his property to Sherman's Army.

Around noon, Hector was led into the woods and shot. When his friends finally found his body, he had thirty-two holes in his chest from shotgun-slugs and assorted bullets. The back of the body was too mangled to count the exit wounds.

CHAPTER 10

Elizabeth and Neil had almost fallen asleep in their bedroom when they heard a commotion downstairs. Ben and some unknown men were yelling at one another at the back of the house. Something large crashed to the floor.

Neil was quick to get out of bed, grab his gun belt, and strap it around his waist as he rushed toward sounds of a scuffle on the first floor. Elizabeth had tried to hold him back, but her husband was out of the room before she could speak.

Once at the bottom of the staircase on the ground floor, Neil could make out men silhouetted in darkness by the moonlight of the open back door as they knocked Ben to the floor and burst their way into the kitchen of his home.

The invaders were yelling and trying to intimidate anyone who may be in the house. However, Colonel McRae was not a man to be intimidated, especially in his own home!

Without saying a word, the Colonel pulled his service revolver and fired twice at the silhouettes as they dove for cover, the bullets missing the intruders and smashing through the glass panes of the back door.

Much to Colonel McRae's surprise, the kitchen seemed to light up as guns went off in the darkness. Why they were shooting back at him? In his own house! Was this a robbery or could it be Yankee troops?

Without waiting to find out, the Colonel ran back up the stairs to gain a better defensive position so he could protect his wife. But there was little worry there because as soon as he was at the top of the stairs, Elizabeth met him with a shotgun in her hands. Together they positioned themselves at angles to shoot anyone who showed himself.

They could hear the men below rushing to get out of the house and into positions outside that gave them better cover. The gunfight continued.

Neil told Elizabeth to lie down at the top of the stairs and shoot anyone that appeared on the stairway. Then, he disappeared back into their bedroom and went to a window that looked out over the back of their property. He opened the room's window and began to shoot at anything he thought to be one of the intruders. So many shots were fired it sounded as if the war had begun anew at Argyle Manor.

Despite what she'd been told, Elizabeth made her way down the stairs to the first floor. Moving from shadow to shadow, she found her way to the back of the house and to the kitchen. There, she found Ben unconscious on the floor. She moved to the open back door and onto the back porch. Beside the steps, bathed in moonlight, she could plainly see Henry Berry Lowrie standing there, looking her directly in the eyes. His shotgun pointed at her midsection. When Henry didn't shoot Elizabeth raised her shotgun, pointed it at Henry Berry and pulled both triggers.

"Click-Click"

Both shotgun barrels were empty.

In her haste, Elizabeth had picked up the shotgun unaware it wasn't loaded.

Henry Berry lowered his own shotgun, walked off toward the tool sheds and disappeared into the dense dark woods that surrounded the estate. The shooting stopped, and the only thing Elizabeth could hear was the silence of the night.

That silence was broken when Edith cried out for Ben, as she ran to him from their back bedroom. She lit a lantern and looked her husband over quickly to find only scrapes, bruises, and a large bump on the back of his head.

Elizabeth made sure no intruders remained on the porch before she closed and locked the back door. She left Ben and Edith to clean up the broken glass and pots scattered across the floor. Her bedroom slippers made no sound as she headed up the stairs to her bedroom. The stairs creaked where the boards were slightly loose.

At the top of the stairs, she called, "Neil, where are you?" There was no reply, and her blood froze.

On a table outside their bedroom, she found a hurricane lantern, lit it, and held it away from her to maximize the light. She slowly entered her room, watching the light cast shadows that seemed to run along the walls and floor like mischievous goblins. Fear gripped her and she couldn't breathe. As she came to the window where Neil had stationed himself, she found him slumped against the wall.

Trembling, she moved the light over him as though she did not wish to disturb his slumber. As the light moved closer, chasing away the last shadows, she could see a bullet hole through the wall by the open window and another bullet hole in the left side of Neil's chest. Blood ran down his side and collected in an ever-growing dark pool.

As if she were in a dream, she set the lantern on the dressing table next to the wall and slowly sat down beside her husband. She placed his head in her lap. She leaned over and put her head against Neil's forehead and began to rock back and forth in disbelief.

First, Harlee, now Neil. She felt for all the world she was now alone. Tears welled up in her eyes and flowed down her face. All she could whisper was, "No. No. No. No. No. No. No. No. No."

God had truly forsaken them.

CHAPTER 11

Tensions were running near the boiling point when the Lumberton town crier shouted out the news: "All slaves henceforth are FREED!"

The news was met with gritted teeth by the white citizens who vowed revenge against those they had enslaved.

More bitterness came with the news that President Johnson required that North Carolina repeal its 1861 Ordinance of Secession and ratify the Thirteenth Amendment that *abolished slavery and involuntary servitude, except as punishment for a crime.*

But for the freed blacks, it was a time to rejoice! Celebrations spontaneously broke out among all the blacks for the Lord had kept his promise!

Halleluiah!

For the local Indians, there was no reason to celebrate. They were already considered *Free Blacks* even though they were not black. But, that was how the whites wished to see them—on the same socio-economic level as blacks. They were not considered citizens. They could not vote, they could not go to school, and were at a loss as to what changes they might see now that the war was over.

For the whites, it seemed that God had abandoned their cause and that the North sought to embarrass and belittle the once proud Rebels.

On May 15, Confederate President Jefferson Davis was reported to have finally been captured in Georgia, and the Yankees made sure all the local newspaper reports from the arresting Yankee troops stated that President Davis had been captured *wearing a woman's skirt and shawl.* Worse still, Davis was being held in a small cell, chained to his bed, with a BLACK Union Soldier guarding his door!

The humiliation heaped upon the once great Confederate States caused the Southern Conservatives to HATE the Federal Government even more; if that was possible.

It seemed the North wanted the South to wallow and suffer in its defeat. Perhaps the damn Yankees did intend to make the blacks masters of the white citizens? Perhaps the Union, under martial law, would carve up the plantations and give land to the former slaves?

Elizabeth McRae, for one, would see that her family was avenged for the harm they had suffered. She aligned herself with her powerful friends, such as the Norments, and they offered the sheriff $300 as a reward for Henry Berry Lowrie.

Sheriff King already had 35 outstanding warrants against Henry Berry Lowrie for robbery and burglary. Elizabeth and Mary wanted those warrants to include MURDER even though no one had actually seen Henry Berry commit any killings.

With everything in near ruin and disarray, unemployment and starvation was a very real problem for most average citizens, and not just the blacks and Indians.

A $300 reward would be mighty tempting to any bounty hunter willing to go into the swamps after Henry Berry Lowrie.

Elizabeth was told by her friends that word was going around that Henry Berry, the Lowries, and their gang members were considered to be Robin Hood-like heroes to the locals because without the gang's help many families would have starved during the lean final year of the war.

Elizabeth and Mary convinced their friends that the gang, and especially Henry Berry Lowrie, must only be reported in newspapers as murderous thugs and robbers. The last thing they wanted was for these Indian outlaws to be held up as champions.

Adjusted for inflation
$300 of 1865 dollars
is worth $4,494 in 2018

1866

Love is the ultimate outlaw.

It just won't adhere to any rules.

The most any of us can do

is sign on as its accomplice.

Instead of vowing

to honor and obey,

maybe we should swear

to aid and abet.

Tom Robbins

Total documented raids on local Plantations by the Lowrie Gang
in **1866 = 0**

CHAPTER 12

Union troops came to North Carolina to ensure a smooth transition from war to peace with their attempt at what was called Reconstruction. However, the Radicals in Congress believed that Congress, *not* the President, should have the final say on when and how the Southern States should be readmitted into the Union.

North Carolina and the other Southern States quickly enacted laws that restricted blacks from assembling without a white man present, from traveling freely, from voting, and from owning guns. Public facilities were segregated between whites and persons of color. Most challenging for the newly freed blacks were new vagrancy laws that stated if a person of color was not employed and did not own land, they faced the possibility of arrest.

These new laws were called Black Codes, and they were the attempts by whites to keep the freedmen subservient. Although the Southern whites accepted the abolition of slavery, most did not see persons of color as their equals. Nonwhites were still at the bottom of the social order. The Southern whites believed that, if left alone, the blacks would find their natural place in society; meaning they would always be subservient to the whites.

In response to the South's Black Codes, the Radicals in Washington passed the Fourteenth Amendment. President Johnson vetoed it, but the Radicals overrode the veto. This Constitutional Amendment guaranteed that freedmen were extended full rights as citizens of the United States, and disallowed re-admittance into the Union of any Southern State that denied former slaves the right to vote.

The North Carolina delegation refused to ratify the Fourteenth Amendment. The result was that it would take another two-and-a-half years of Yankee occupation before North Carolina would finally capitulate and be reinstated into the Union.

The new Radical Reconstruction plans for North Carolina brought in diverse people to help rebuild and reorganize the South. The Freedman Bureau was established for the purpose of acclimating and resettling the newly freed black population. Their mission was to help distribute food to the needy, to help establish schools to educate blacks and help them obtain abandoned land.

Based on appearances, peace seemed to return. All was deemed forgotten, and all war crimes were dismissed. It was time for everyone to move on.

For the Indians, though, life was still difficult. They were not reimbursed for goods stolen or commandeered by Sherman's Army, as were the white citizens who usually lied and padded their claims to make them worth more than was actually due.

The Indians seemed to take this in stride and returned to their peaceful ways, to live and let live. With the Union troops enforcing martial law, no one seemed genuinely interested in coming after the Lowries in hopes of collecting a reward.

During the summer of 1866, Henry and his brothers and friends cleared land just south of The Settlement, across the river and surrounded by dense woodland. The Lowries were expert woodworkers and craftsman by trade. Building a house for Henry Berry was a labor of love. One evening when Henry and Rhoda were watching the sunset behind the Strong's home, Henry asked Rhoda to be his wife. At first, when she turned her back, Henry thought he was going to be turned down.

In fact, Rhoda had turned away quickly to hide her immense joy! She was so happy she was afraid her heart would jump out of her chest. When she finally turned back toward Henry, no words were necessary; the twinkle in her eyes and her big smile said it all—Yes!

Finally, the world was sane again, and they would have a family of their own. Thank God!

Their wedding day finally arrived on December 7, 1866. The ceremony was held in the front yard of Pollie's house. It seemed that everyone from near and far surrounding The Settlement were there for the joyous event. Everyone was dressed to the nines in their Sunday-best clothing. Cutout paper flowers were everywhere. There was a 35-foot table, covered with tablecloths and laden with the food everyone had brought to add to the feast and the celebration of life. Most of the Lowrie brothers were musicians, and there was much dancing and gaiety. Finally, there was a reason to celebrate.

A white neighbor and friend, Hector J. McLean, Esq., presented the vows and beamed with approval as the groom kissed the bride. Then, to his embarrassment, his stomach growled loudly. It seemed H. J. McLean, Esq., hadn't eaten in a while, either.

Everyone was having a grand time when suddenly the laughter and merriment died off. The music stopped.

A former member of the Home Guard, Lieutenant A. J. McNair, who was Major O. C. Norment's nephew, had appeared with a posse of twenty armed men. They were there to arrest Henry Berry Lowrie. McNair held out thirty-five old warrants for robbery that Henry snatched from his hand.

The men of the posse tensed and placed thumbs on gun stock hammers. Everyone froze in place. No one moved a muscle.

Rhoda could see Henry Berry's eyes once again going to black, and she feared her new husband would be killed on their wedding day. His first response was to yell at the men to *get the hell off his land* as he began tensing up for a fight.

To help ease the tension, Lieutenant McNair dismounted and walked before Henry Berry and Rhoda and apologized for his uninvited presence. Then he asked, in a most respectful and polite manner, for Henry to come along with them. He didn't come to cause trouble.

The Lieutenant told Henry that he was to take him into custody by order of the High Sheriff, Reuben King, who Henry knew to be one of the wealthiest plantation owners in the state. The man was also a bigot, racist, money-grabbing bastard. They'd met a couple times before, and history did not favor a friendship between the two men.

Henry looked at the faces of his family, friends, and neighbors and understood that if a fight broke out here, many innocents would be hurt, perhaps killed.

Rhoda, as usual, spoke her mind clearly. She felt Henry should go. "Better to fight this matter in a court of law than to start a public killing that would stop when and where? With your death? Bear, these men will get their reward money whether they take you dead or alive. You know that. You ain't going to jilt *me*, **MR. LOWRIE**! I married you, and now you're going to fulfill those vows. Got it?"

Rhoda and Pollie made Henry Berry turn to face them both. Their faces spoke of dangers to so many innocents at their gathering. Rhody smiled, and the love in her eyes for her man caused Henry's eyes to dissolve back to their pure blue color. He could see the hope and desperation in her declaration, the strength in her eyes as they filled with tears. But she would not allow one teardrop to flow down her cheeks. She would not give this *citizens' posse* that pleasure.

Henry could feel his heart swell, and once again, he realized he loved her more than his own life. She *was* his life. She was his *WIFE!* He understood the wisdom of Rhody's words. He couldn't start his marriage with bloodshed, nor could he live his life as a man on the run.

Mr. Henry Berry Lowrie, husband, told the lieutenant that he would go along with them, but in doing so voluntarily, there was no need to put him in irons. It was a small gesture.

The small group of men followed Henry off the property and out of sight. Their destination? The jailhouse in Lumberton.

CHAPTER 13

The posse marched Henry Berry down the lane to Deep Branch Road and then onto Oxendine Road, which they followed to the train depot at New Hope Junction. The train was still at the station huffing and puffing like an impatient dragon. The conductor called out, "All aboard!"

Lieutenant A. J. McNair and three of his deputies escorted Henry Berry Lowrie into the last passenger car, which was located just before the caboose. The lieutenant then dismissed the remainder of his posse with orders to leave their horses at the New Hope livery stables to be picked up upon their return that evening.

Lieutenant McNair sat Henry Berry down and then sat beside him on the bench. One of his deputies sat across from the two, facing them on the adjacent bench. The other two deputies stood at opposite ends of the passenger car and guarded the exits.

Other than traveling through a rather violent thunderstorm, the trip was uneventful. No one felt like talking. When the train finally stopped at the train depot at Elm Street in Lumberton, the storm had passed, and the clouds were breaking up to reveal blue skies.

The small group of men walked behind Henry Berry as they passed a barbershop across the street to their right. On their side of Elm Street, they walked along the wooden sidewalks passing several two-story brick buildings; a general merchandise, a grocery store, and a printing shop. They couldn't avoid the mud in the road when the sidewalks ended at each block. All the men could do was try to avoid the deepest standing water left by the storm. By the time they crossed Elm Street onto

Court House Square, everyone's boots were covered in mud and manure.

Once back onto a sidewalk, each man skidded, stomped, and hopped off as much of the muck as possible. Whatever remained on their shoes would dry to a grey crust.

The Lumberton Jail was located on the second floor of the Robeson County Courthouse, a large, square, red brick, three-story building with towering white columns facing south on Elm Street. The building sat in the middle of the block surrounded by a nicely cut green lawn. This particular real estate was located in the very center of town, and even without the letters above the four white columns, CITY HALL, the architecture of the building stated the place was utilitarian and government operated. In other words, Henry Berry Lowrie was about to enter bureaucratic hell.

As they approached the entrance to the courthouse, the sounds of saws and hammers drifted out of the building as workmen scurried in and out like so many ants.

Entering the building from the South Court Square, the small group of men had to step aside in order to give right-of-way to a pair of carpenter's helpers as they moved freshly cut timbers through the hallway and up the stairs to the second floor. The group followed them up the stairs to where the sheriff's office and jails were located. The entire building smelled of fresh-cut wood. For a jail, the scent was rather refreshing.

At the top of the stairs, the second floor opened up to sawdust-covered floors. To the left, down the hall, the last door on the right, they found the sheriff's office for Robeson County. The door was closed, so Lieutenant McNair knocked before entering. From inside the room, they heard a gruff commanding voice growl, "Come in!"

McNair opened the door and let it swing wide open. He then stepped aside and nodded his head to motion for Henry Berry Lowrie to enter the room. Henry Berry walked in and stood before the Sheriff's desk, which was at the far end of the room facing the doorway.

The big man sitting behind the desk was the High Sheriff of Robeson County, Reuben King, the county's longtime High Sheriff who not only ran Lumberton but the entire county. He remained one of the wealthiest men in the state because he'd diversified his holdings into land, gold, silver and English investments, instead of putting his entire fortune into slaves. He was a smart, devious man, controlling much of the tobacco, pine lumber, and turpentine market because he never trusted that cotton would remain a wonder cash crop. Cotton just required too much manual labor for his liking.

Sheriff King, like most of the big plantation owners, viewed the Indians as a lower class than the blacks, not just because they were poor but also because they tended to be rather disrespectful of authority. At least the blacks understood their social position, free or not.

"Why isn't this man in irons?" barked the High Sheriff.

"Well, sir, he said he'd come quiet if we didn't handcuff him and he done just that, came along real nice and peaceful like," the lieutenant quickly added.

"Townsend! Get in here!" shouted Sheriff King.

Deputy Townsend walked across the hall from his office and leaned into King's office, "Yes, sir?"

"Get some handcuffs and leg irons and see that this prisoner is made comfortable," ordered King.

Henry Berry and Sheriff King locked eyes in a staring contest.

The sheriff finally blinked as he looked down and opened the top drawer of his desk, reached in and pulled out a Navy Colt Revolver. He looked hard into Henry Berry's eyes again and then set the gun on the desk in front of him, his hand snug around the pistol grip. The business end of the weapon was pointed directly at the center of Henry Berry's chest. Henry took note.

Everyone who'd entered the room and was standing behind Lowrie also took note and moved to either side of him so as not to be in the line of fire, just in case.

"We ain't gonna have any problems today, are we now, Mr. Lowrie?" the Sheriff said with just a hint of a smirk on his lips.

"There's no need for irons," Henry stated flatly again. "I came of my own free will to settle this matter."

"Well, that's good to know because I'd just as soon you give me a reason to shoot you right here and now," whispered Sheriff King.

Henry Berry sat very still, but King could see the muscles in his jaw twitching with rage, the only indication that he wasn't as calm as a man watching a peaceful sunset.

Deputy Townsend came into the room carrying handcuffs and leg irons.

"Those aren't needed," Henry Berry said a final time.

"Oh, indeed they are. It's department policy to restrain all murderers and thugs," Sheriff King said gruffly, spitting his words through clenched teeth. Everyone noticed the Sheriff's eyes narrow, and his gaze became that of a predator.

Startled by the sheriff's statement, Henry Berry was incredulous, "What do you mean murderer? Who am I supposed to have killed?"

"Well, besides three dozen outstanding warrants for theft and robbery, I also have here a warrant for your arrest for the murder of James P. Barnes," stated the sheriff, matter-of-factly.

"That's just wrong. I've never killed anyone! *Especially* my old neighbor Mr. Barnes. We all got along just fine," insisted Henry Berry.

"We'll allow the court to decide the matter. Deputy put this man in irons," ordered the High Sheriff.

Deputy Townsend walked over to where Henry Berry was sitting and dropped the leg irons on the floor next to the Indian. He and Henry Berry looked at each other as they each took a deep breath and sighed in resignation. Neither man was left with much of a choice, though one of them was *really* not at all satisfied with the results. The Deputy took hold of Henry's right wrist and snapped the handcuff closed. He did the same thing with Henry's left wrist. Then the deputy installed the leg irons and inspected the locks on the chains between Henry Berry's ankles to ensure they were securely locked, as well.

"Is there anything else, Sheriff?" Deputy Townsend asked in a way that almost made him sound tuckered out from the effort.

"No, go back to what you were doing," mumbled the High Sheriff, trying to read Henry Berry's expressionless eyes. The man had an excellent poker face, the sheriff thought. Though intuitively, he understood that behind the mask was raw courage, the likes of which he'd never seen. The sheriff could feel it in his gut. The man sitting across from him was not to be trusted. This was a dangerous man.

It was no secret to the white man that blacks *understood* that they were socially submissive to whites. They dared not fight, or they would be hunted down and hanged. But these same white men also realized that the Indians, especially in the swamps and backwoods, were a different problem entirely. You couldn't just fight *one* of these Indians; they were like a hornet's nest, in that when one was attacked, they ALL attacked with family, cousins, and close friends joining in. Yet, what troubled the white men of the area the most was the knowledge that these Indians just wouldn't *fight fair*!

A cut piece of lumber fell loudly to the floor not far from the sheriff's office sounding like a gunshot. Henry Berry didn't move. The sheriff hoped no one noticed his ever so slight jitter as he realized he'd almost pulled the trigger.

The moment snapped him out of his stupor and, using a different tone of voice in order to enhance his finest Charleston Southern accent, continued what he was saying. "Unfortunately, MISTER Lowrie, our accommodations are somewhat lacking at this time, as you can see from the dust and construction. Though you can rest assured, we're expanding our jails to accommodate more of your kind. So please excuse our lack of hospitality. I can assure you, it's only temporary."

King looked away from Henry Berry and spoke directly to Lieutenant McNair, "Take the prisoner over to Whitesville Jail. They're expecting him."

"When do we get our reward?" asked the lieutenant.

"When you fucking get the prisoner safely delivered and locked up over at Whitesville! Now, ya'll get the hell out of my office. I've got too much damn paperwork to do to listen to your whining!" said King in a condescending tone. Then he added, "Here, take your prisoner delivery papers to the County Clerk's Office, tomorrow. Don't forget to have the Whitesville jailer complete his portion of the bill of lading or the clerk won't accept it. And 'no,' I don't know *when* you get your money. That's not part of my jurisdiction."

"Yes sir," the lieutenant half muttered under his breath. "Come on, Lowrie. Let's get going."

Henry Berry's eyes were still locked on the High Sheriff. Slowly, he got up from his chair, the heavy chains rattling as he moved.

"You got anything more to say, Lowrie?" hissed the Sheriff.

"Sure. You can kiss my ass!"

The small posse escorted Henry Berry Lowrie back down the stairs and made him wait while one of the deputies requisitioned a wagon and horses to make the thirty-mile trip to Whitesville, traveling southeast of Lumberton down the Andrew Jackson Highway. They would have to maintain a reasonably brisk pace if they hoped to be back at New Hope Station before dark.

CHAPTER 14

Henry Berry sat in the middle of the flatbed of the open wagon with his back against the driver's seat, his legs straight out. The position was dreadfully uncomfortable, but Henry refused to acknowledge his discomfort because he didn't want his captors to see he was in pain. Instead, he focused his attention on the spinning wagon wheels that would hurl an occasional glob of muck over the sides of the wagon, eventually covering the guards' coats and hats with the stuff the further they traveled down the muddy roads.

As Henry Berry bounced about uncomfortably, he couldn't help but smile with the realization that he was clean and dry; a small victory. They may be winning this game, he thought, but seeing his guards covered in slop certainly made him feel better.

The afternoon sun was just beginning its slide toward the western horizon, forcing long shadows to reach out from the Whitesville Jail toward them as the open wagon rattled to a halt. The horses snorted their objections.

The guards hopped off the back of the wagon, the last man off offering Henry Berry a hand to help him off the flatbed. The gesture was accepted and much appreciated because Henry's legs were numb from the ride. Henry tried to stamp some blood back into his feet, causing his chains to rattle and shoot pain into his ankles and up his legs as the metal bindings dug into his flesh.

Lieutenant McNair dismounted from his horse and handed the reins to the first muddy guardsman he passed on the way to the jail entrance. The rest of the men followed along behind Henry's hobbling pace.

Each step caused the metal bindings to cut a little deeper into the flesh of Henry Berry's ankles. "You couldn't have pulled that wagon just a little closer to the door, could you Lieutenant?" deadpanned Lowrie.

The lieutenant didn't reply but opened the heavy door of another red brick building that looked like a cross between a warehouse and a fortress. His boots echoed off the wooden floors as he walked toward a small barred window at the end of the hallway. If you didn't know better, you'd think he was going to a teller's window at the bank.

McNair slid his copies of the prisoner delivery papers under the window bars to the man on the other side. That man looked over the lieutenant's shoulder to take a good look at the prisoner before unfolding the documents. Once satisfied with his view of the prisoner, he read the papers.

"Looks here like this warrant is dated December 8. Today is the 7th," noted the Jailer.

McNair became quite indignant and pleaded, "Well, it's late in the day, and we just came all the way from Scuffletown by way of Lumberton, and I'm in no mood to take the prisoner back and do this over again tomorrow! He's a criminal, and you need to lock him up today!"

The jailer gave no sign of reaction to McNair's demand. He just sort of nodded and walked out of sight to unlock the door to the jailhouse holding area.

McNair said he needed the prisoner delivery papers signed and his copies returned to him.

The jailer told him, "You'll get those once the prisoner is delivered, meaning locked in a cell."

The group walked down another hallway to the bottom of a stairwell and waited for the jailer to close and lock the only exit door. As the jailer walked toward the head of the group, he realized they could hear a woman's voice from the other side of the hallway wall. "My family lives in an apartment under the cells. It helps ensure full-time security of the premises. We're quite proud to say we've *never* had a prisoner successfully break out of our jail," noted the jailer as he began his ascent up the stairway to the floor above.

The staircase itself was an alarm system because each footfall on a wooden step caused the boards to screech and scrape as though in agony under their weight. It was the kind of sound that would wake a dead man in the middle of the night.

At the top of the stairway, the wooden floor extended down the corridor with five cells along each side. The cells were separated by brick walls with iron bars forming the wall facing the center walkway. The rear wall was also brick with a barred open window overlooking the surrounding courtyard. The floors in the open corridor made the same loud annoying sounds as the stairs.

Henry Berry followed the jailer past one empty cell after another. At the end of the long hall, the jailer pulled open the door on the last cell on the left side of the room. Henry was led over to sit on the bed located against the wall opposite the cell's entrance.

The Jailer told the lieutenant to remove the leg irons. The lieutenant seemed to hesitate, so the jailer added, "Ain't nobody escaped from this jail and my wife won't be able to sleep if the prisoner is dragging these heavy chains across this wooden floor above our sleeping quarters. Take the leg irons off, at least. I don't care about the chain between his wrists."

The lieutenant nodded to the deputy holding the keys, and the man removed Henry's leg irons. Henry Berry held both arms out and looked innocently at the lieutenant, smiling.

"Leave the wrist-chains on," stated the Lieutenant in a flat tone, "I intend to collect our reward."

"What time is dinner served, jailer?" inquired Henry Berry with a hint of charm.

"Tomorrow morning." chuckled, the jailer.

Without further dialog, the group exited the cell. The jailer locked fast the cell door, and the group walked back down the hallway, accompanied by the hardwood floor's chorus of squeaks. From the bottom of the stairwell, the lieutenant shouted, "By the way, congratulations on your marriage! A lovely girl. Enjoy your honeymoon!"

The sound of men laughing faded after the exit door shut and the bolt slammed into place.

Henry reached down and massaged his raw ankles while looking at the room's décor. The room was bare except for a shit-bucket in the corner and a metal bed frame covered by a mattress that reeked of urine. At the foot of the bed was a neatly folded brown woolen blanket. Henry took the blanket off the mattress and threw the mattress over by the cell's front wall of bars. He then unfolded the blanket on the bed frame and lay back, swinging his legs up. There was nothing to do but hurry up and wait.

The next day, Henry Berry was up with the sun and grumpy from feeling hungry for too long. He knew not to yell down to the deputy that he was hungry because that would only slow the deputy down. So, to quiet his rumbling stomach, Henry reached into his coat pocket and found a small lump of chewing tobacco. Chewing tobacco was an old Indian method to ward off hunger. Of course, the real trick was not swallowing the wad.

Though if he did accidentally swallow the wad, he'd feel so sick he wouldn't feel like eating, which was almost as good as not being hungry. He was always appreciative of the small gifts in life.

Eventually, sounds of keys entering locks and bolts being thrown followed by the sounds of a door opening, then different wood squeaks as the deputy climbed the noisy stairs to the second floor. The sounds of his footsteps and squeaking boards announced his progress to the cell where the only prisoner waited.

Henry Berry was sitting on the bed with his back against the brick wall. He didn't have to try to look bored. He leaned forward, hopped off the bed and stretched his arms out wide until they reached the length of the chain connecting his handcuffs and, acting like he just noticed his bindings, asked the deputy if he could kindly remove the restrictions.

Ignoring the prisoner's plea, the deputy unlocked and pulled open the jail door with one hand and handed Henry Berry a breakfast tray with his other. The meal consisted of a plate of scrambled eggs, a piece of hardtack likely left over from the war and a cup of warm black coffee.

Before leaving, the deputy looked into the shit bucket and was pleased to see it empty. Satisfied that everything was in order, the deputy walked out of the cell, locked the door behind him and made his squeaky exit. Quiet returned to the upper floor once the last bolt slammed shut and the jailhouse was once more secure.

For Henry Berry, the day seemed to move along at the speed of grass growing. Once an hour, the key to the jail door would be heard to open the latch, the door bolt shot open and the door hinges would creak, followed by the squeaking boards under the pressure of each footfall announcing the jailer's progress to Henry Berry's cell.

Around noon, much to Henry's surprise, the jailer told him lunch would be delivered to him at the next hourly check. He hadn't expected lunch, so that was a pleasant surprise, but he never imagined he'd have dessert, too.

CHAPTER 15

Rhoda had planned to take the train into Lumberton thinking Henry Berry was incarcerated in the town jail. Fortunately for her, on the evening of the wedding, Hector McLean happened to cross paths with a Lumberton deputy from whom he learned of Henry Berry's actual location. Upon learning this, Hector went straight to The Settlement to let the New Hope Church preacher know so the information could be delivered to Rhoda and Pollie Lowrie. Hector had given a time when he'd return the next day to take Rhoda in his horse and buggy to Whitesville. He knew Rhoda would get his message and she'd be waiting for him when he arrived the next day. The efficiency and speed of the Indian grapevine never ceased to amaze him.

When they arrived at the Whitesville Jail, it was mid-afternoon. Hector escorted Mrs. Rhoda Lowrie into the jailhouse. At the main door with the barred window, Hector picked up the handbell and rang it several times to make the jailer aware of their presence. Shortly, the jailer came forward from his living quarters and greeted the pair, "Good afternoon."

"Good afternoon," replied Mr. McLean. "We are here to see Mr. Lowrie."

"Ah, yes. Mr. Lowrie is well and waiting upstairs. But, what's the cake for?" asked the jailer.

"The lady with me is the newlywed, Mrs. Henry Berry Lowrie, and she's brought her new husband one of their wedding cakes," stated Mr. McLean, matter-of-factly.

"Well, I don't know. What kind of a fool do you think I am? There might be a file in that cake. I've heard that one, before," the jailer said, concerned it could be true.

"Why sir, if you'll bring some plates and forks, I'd be pleased for you to share some cake with us. Then you'll see there is no file inside," cooed Rhody with just a hint of flirting in her eyes.

The old jailer smiled and melted under the spell of such a lovely lady's charm.

"Can I bring my wife up, too? She loves cake!"

"I'd be delighted to meet your wife, and she can have as much cake as she likes," said Rhoda with an almost girlish giggle.

The jailer disappeared. A muffled conversation could be heard through the walls, but the words were not loud enough to be understood.

A door at the end of the hallway opened, and the jailer appeared. "This way, folks, Mr. Lowrie is in one of our 2nd-floor suites. Please follow me." offered the jailer with a chuckle at his own wit.

At first, Henry Berry was just going to continue to lie on his bed as he listened to the floorboards squeak, but this time he heard voices, so he sat up and looked at the cell door.

As soon as he saw Rhoda, he jumped off the cot and shouted, "Rhody!"

She handed off the cake to Hector and ran to her husband. They kissed through the cell bars and never once thought to wait for the jailer to open the door.

The jailer was all smiles as he approached the door and told Rhoda to move aside while he unlocked the door so she could enter. But, before he opened the door, he told Henry Berry to walk to the other side of his cell, away from the door. No one had ever escaped from Whitesville Jail, and Henry wasn't going to be the first.

Henry moved back and sat on the bed, admiring how pretty Rhoda looked. She had on a lovely blue dress that came all the way down to her ankles. There was white lace around the collar and cuffs. Her long black hair framed her face like a picture. Her smile lit up the room.

Henry had never seen the dress before but understood without asking that, like most of the women in and around The Settlement, these clothes were taken from the plantations, booty from the gang's raids. However, there was little chance that the original owner would recognize the dress now because the women would take several dresses, disassemble the pieces of cloth and sew themselves a new tailor-made dress. The parts of the old dresses that weren't used were either traded with the other women or made into clothing for the children.

The jailer opened the door and stood aside to allow Rhoda to walk inside Henry's cell, closing and locking the door behind her.

Rhoda and Henry kissed again, but Henry abruptly stopped and held his arms out toward the jailer and asked, "Can you please take these cuffs off so I can hug my new wife properly?"

"Nope," was all the jailer said, as squeaking steps announced someone else coming up from downstairs.

"Ah, Helen!" said the jailer, "Come on over and meet the newlyweds, Mr. and Mrs. Lowrie."

"Hey," said Helen, who was now close enough to see the newlyweds were paying them no attention.

Henry had lifted his shackled wrists above Rhoda's head and brought his arms down behind her so they could embrace properly, with impassioned vigor.

"Oh, my!" blushed Helen, then she said, "Oh, what a lovely cake. It looks delicious."

Hector took that as his cue and said," Who wants some cake?" as he held it out like a prize.

The two men followed the jailer's wife over to the other side of the room, where she placed a set of plates on a table. Hector placed the cake on the table beside the plates.

Helen took out a knife she'd brought up with the plates and forks and sliced the cake into six pieces. She then placed a slice on each of the five dishes, with only one slice left on the original plate. It was apparent there was no file in the cake.

Helen handed a plate with a slice of cake to each man beside her. They stood there for an instant, looked back into the cell where they saw Rhoda sitting on the edge of the bed with her skirt raised to her knees. "You forgot to collect your garter, dear," said Rhody to Henry Berry, who was kneeling before her.

Embarrassed by the display of affection by the newlyweds, the trio turned their backs to give the newlyweds some brief privacy and quickly began some idle chitchat.

Henry looked deep into his new wife's eyes and couldn't believe how they twinkled with joy. Then, he slowly reached his hand under her dress and felt his way up her thigh, higher and higher. But what he found when he reached the garter so shocked him that he looked up, his eyes opened wide, to see Rhoda's twinkling eyes as she looked into his own. "Shhh," Rhoda whispered. "I'll expect you home in a day or so."

Henry Berry's grin told Rhoda all she wished to know as he pulled the garter down her leg and slid the metal file under the blanket on his bed.

CHAPTER 16

Henry Berry had been working the file on the soft iron bars in the window of his cell for about two hours when he heard the lock turn in the jail door downstairs. Soon he could hear the boards squeak their early-warning, which gave him time to put the file back under the blanket and make sure nothing looked amiss. Then he walked over to the cell door to wait for the jailer. He wanted the jailer to focus on him and not the cell window where he'd been working.

The two made small talk about how beautiful Rhoda was and how good her cake was. Security check complete, the jailer returned downstairs.

A few hours later, the jailer returned for a final nighttime security check. As the jailer walked across the squeaky floors, long shadowy apparitions danced silently about the walls and ceiling caused by the light of the kerosene lantern the jailer held ahead of him. He completed his nightly rounds to ensure the jail was secure for the night.

As the creaking boards accompanied the retreating shadows down the stairs, Henry Berry yelled out to the jailer, "Good night and sleep tight!" No reply from downstairs other than the exit door closing at the foot of the stairs and the lock's bolt slamming shut, secure for the night.

Sometime around 3:00 a.m., Henry finished filing through a second window bar, which provided just enough room for him to squeeze through. Before going outside, Henry tore off a section of the blanket and wrapped it around the chain connecting his wrists to keep them silent. Then he tied the remainder of the blanket to the remaining window bar to use as a rope to lower him down to freedom.

After a moment to prepare mentally, he took in a deep breath, let out a very long deep sigh, then inhaled again deeply and pulled himself up onto the windowsill and slid his feet through the hole in the wall.

Eventually, he was able to work himself down the blanket against the wall. He took another deep breath, pushed himself away from the wall, checked his balance as he fell, bent his knees and dropped to his feet in the soft grass surrounding the building, doing a back roll to dispel the energy from his impact. As he rolled to his feet, he popped up into a standing crouch position and froze in place.

He stood motionless for some time and just listened, but heard nothing. His eyes adjusted to the dark of night and he held tightly to the swath of blanket wrapped around the chain between his wrists and swiftly disappeared into the starlit December night.

He stayed in the shadows as he made his way back toward The Settlement. He figured he was about 45, maybe 50 miles, from his new house and new bride. It might take him all night and day to get there, but get there he would. First, he needed to find a livery stable, blacksmith shop or someplace to find a hammer and chisel to break apart the old iron handcuffs around his wrists.

Not too far up the road, he came to a stable on the far side of a pasture. In the starlight, he could see well enough once inside the building to see that one stall was used as a blacksmith area. There, on an old oak stump that was used as a woodblock - was the hammer and chisel he needed.

He placed his left wrist against the woodblock and inserted the chisel between the left-side lock where the handcuffs linked up around his wrist. He needed to adjust the handcuff band around his wrist so he could hold the chisel with his left hand and strike the chisel with his right.

Before he struck the chisel, he wrapped part of the blanket swath around it to quiet the strike. On the third strike, the lock popped open and freed his arm. He set down the hammer and rubbed his sore wrist to encourage his blood to flow through. After a moment, he felt better and repeated the process on the cuff around his right wrist. This time the effort required five strikes, but the job was done, and he was again a free man.

He headed due west until he came to the Lumber River, what the locals called Drowning Creek. Then, he followed the river north until he found a rowboat tied to a small dock. Both the dock and rowboat were old, and half rotted away. The bottom of the boat was filled with stagnant water, which Henry bailed out with his cupped hands as best he could.

There were no oars, so he lay across the bow and used his hands as paddles. The slow current took him southward with the boat taking on water. By the time he reached the opposite riverbank, water had filled the bottom of the boat and his shoes. But he was across the river, the only major obstacle between him and Rhoda.

His luck held out as he passed a settlement of houses. He found a blanket draped over an outside clothesline, which he wrapped around his shoulders to keep out the chilly night air. Better still, he discovered three pies on a kitchen windowsill, obviously forgotten by an absentminded cook. As hungry as Henry Berry was, he only took one pie. He was an outlaw, not a pie thief.

Once he was in an area of woods far from houses, he made a small fire. The heat from the fire and tasty apple pie satisfied him so much he lay down next to the fire and took a nap. He awoke with the sun's warmth on his face and felt reenergized in his determination to get home to his new wife, as fast as possible, while avoiding detection.

He walked and jogged all day, and arrived at his cabin hidden in the woods sometime after dark. From the edge of the property, he called out for Rhoda. No reply came. He moved through the shadows and across the yard until he was at a tree beside the house. He again called out for Rhody. This time she had no doubt who was calling her name. She came bounding out the front door only to be momentarily confused because there was no one to be found.

Henry Berry stepped out of the shadows behind her and whispered, "Hey, Sweetheart! Ya miss me?"

She turned and pounced on him and wrapped her arms around his chest and screamed happily, "My husband has returned!"

Henry brought his arms around her and hugged her tightly. They held each other for what never seemed long enough. Finally, Rhoda pulled back. They absentmindedly reached up to touch the kiss lingering on their lips and burst out laughing at the perfect synchronizations of their movements in the starlight.

"Hey, I could get used to this!" he laughed.

"Likely the best way to keep you under control, my dear husband," quipped Rhody.

For a while, they just stood outside their house and held each other tightly. Rhoda could smell Henry's journey - which was of campfire smoke, pine bedding, peat moss, and earth: to her, *he smelled like home.*

She also realized he reeked of very pungent body odor after two days on the run. Releasing her hug ever so slightly, she looked up into his eyes, "Bear, we need to get you a bath. You stink!" As always, she'd dismissed everything inconsequential and shot straight to the matter at hand.

Henry Berry adored his lifelong friend and scooped his bride up in his arms, and carried her back to their new home, up the front steps, across the wood porch, through the doorway and into the main room of the house. To the left was the kitchen and pantry area next to the fireplace used for cooking. Next to the fireplace were the wood stack and the area along the opposite wall that served as their bedroom. In the wall opposite the cooking fireplace was a more prominent fireplace made of stone that was the entire wall. This was the main fireplace that would keep them warm in the coldest of winters. The house still had that pleasant just-cut wood smell. Of course, none of that registered with the newlyweds because they had a lot of honeymooning to catch up on. Made all the sweeter because of the delay, which only served to raise their level of desire and love shared. They would make up for lost time with endless lovemaking.

Now was not the time to talk about their problems with the law. They needed this time to set about making their house a home, as well as a lot more consummating of their marriage!

Eventually, Henry Berry would tell Rhoda the details of his arrest while they lay in the dark beside each other, waiting for sleep. The two lovers drifted off to sleep while spooning, to dream of troubles ahead and boundless hope for a better future.

CHAPTER 17

"**D**amn fools and incompetents!" hissed Elizabeth as she paced about Argyle Manor, the clack of her shoes on the hardwood surface punctuating her words.

"You <u>had</u> the man in shackles but can't keep him in a jail that *is escape-proof*? Well, Whitesville can never make that boast again, can they? Damn him to hell!" she said as she continued to vent and express her utter disdain for those in her employ.

"And, Sheriff King, you better see to it that none of that reward money is paid! The deal is to arrest the Lowries, Oxendines, and the Strongs and anyone else connected with that band of murderers, especially that wily young Henry Berry, and hang the lot!" she demanded, before adding, "Henry Berry may have slipped my grasp this time, but he will pay for what he did to me."

As she spoke, Elizabeth paced about in an uncharacteristic slouch. She seemed smaller, in part, because she held her hands together up against her heart and locked her elbows into her waist. Her shoulders hunched over and she paced the floor as though looking for something lost, allowing her hair to fall into her face untidily.

At that moment, she became aware that she might appear out of character as an aristocratic lady. She straightened her posture, put her shoulders back, and held her head high as she brushed the hair back into place above her eyes. Another moment to take a deep breath and Elizabeth had regained her composure. She sat down on the silk covered couch, crossed her ankles, folded her hands, and smiled. She was still an elegant lady and, in her opinion, she didn't deserve to have life treat her so meanly and unfairly.

"Sheriff King," Elizabeth said in a soft voice that hinted restrained violence, "When I offer a reward, I mean it to be for the capture, holding, legally trying the man, and then seeing him hang!" her voice rising just enough for emphasis, yet within the protocol of Southern politeness: *Bless their hearts.*

Sheriff King reminded Elizabeth, "Yesterday we informed you by telegraph about Henry Berry's capture. Today, Mrs. McRae, out of respect, I came here directly to tell you the news because I wanted to be here to demonstrate to you how disappointed I am in the Whitesville Jail. I promise you I will get Mr. Lowrie for you," added the High Sheriff, with as much empathy, heartfelt commitment, and genuine concern as he could muster with only words and gestures.

Everyone in the Argyle great room understood they were the county's wealthy elite, but what made Mrs. McRae unique in her power was her family's connections. It wasn't what you knew, it was who you knew, and the McRae's had always known the right people. Even the High Sheriff, as wealthy as he was, understood that if he wished to recover from the ruinous lost war, he'd do well to stay on Elizabeth's good side.

1867

Heroes are often the most ordinary of men.

Henry David Thoreau

Total documented raids on local Plantations by the Lowrie Gang

in **1867 = 0**

CHAPTER 18

The actual name of the department set up to administer the Reconstruction Act was the Bureau of Refugees, Freedmen, and Abandoned Lands, but it soon became known as the Freedman's Bureau.

The purpose of the Bureau was not only to help blacks and whites work together, but also to help the former plantation owners rebuild. By signing contracts with their former slaves as employees, the plantations would have their needed labor at a fair market price. Additionally, the Bureau reported to the Secretary of War, who was responsible for the distribution of medicine, clothing, fuel, and food rations to the general population. Most everyone was near destitute from the disastrous war.

The Freedman's Bureau helped newly freed blacks and homeless poor whites to locate abandoned property they could occupy and cultivate as tenant farmers. They were allowed to work on credit and, at the end of the year, the crops they'd grown (usually cotton or tobacco) were harvested and prepared for market to be sold at market value. That money was then deducted from any monies owed. What was left would go to the tenant farmer. Though in reality, the system was rigged so that at the end of the year, the tenant farmer usually owed more than he earned. This meant the tenant often started a new year further in debt.

This was just another way the conservatives manipulated what should have been a good system for helping the poor earn a better life for themselves through their hard work. Instead, it was used by the whites to continue black oppression; without money, there is no power.

Of great importance to the Indians was that the new Radical-controlled state government agreed to look into the killing of Indian men by the Robeson County Home Guard during the war.

CHAPTER 19

Most everyone in the Lowrie and Strong families, along with their friends the Oxendines and Applewhites, were gathered outside the home of the Lowrie matriarch, Pollie. The house was full of women bustling about, chattering non-stop. The men were all outside milling around, trading stories, smoking, chewing tobacco, playing horseshoes, and just biding their time.

As if on cue, the ladies stopped their chatter, and the men stood and looked toward the house. From deep inside the home came the cry of the newest member of the Lowrie family. Rhoda had given birth to a healthy little girl.

Soon Pollie was standing in the doorway with the new bundle of life in her arms to present to the new father. When Henry Berry walked into the house, Pollie handed him his new daughter and introduced them, "Henry Berry, I'd like you to meet your new daughter. Her name is Sally Ann." As they made the exchange, Pollie reminded him to use his arm to cradle the baby and support her head.

Henry's smile was so big it seemed he might burst with joy! He couldn't get over how tiny she was. With his finger, he moved the blanket so he could see her face. Her little hand reached out and grabbed his little finger. She was so small that his finger seemed like a log in her tiny hand.

"Hey! She's got quite a good grip for a girl!" he laughed.

Henry Berry then took the child outside for the first time. All her new uncles, cousins and friends gathered around them like they were huddling to share some grand secret.

George Applewhite spoke first, "She sure is a beautiful little girl. You sure she's yours?"

The remark broke the tension, and everyone laughed and punched George in the arm. Good spirits flowed on a beautiful August day.

Finally, Henry Berry turned and handed his daughter back to her grandma, Pollie.

"Can I see Rhody, now? How's she doing?" he asked Pollie.

"Give her a little while to rest up. She lost a lot of blood, but she'll be alright. Don't you worry about her," Pollie said.

Then Pollie took the baby back inside, and the women all began to fuss over the baby and talk at the same time.

Henry Berry went back outside where his brothers had their instruments. Steven was on the fiddle. Tom was playing the mouth harp, and Henry Berry took up his banjo. The trio played several upbeat tunes that got all the men to dancing.

The crowd stopped dancing, and the music halted when Pollie appeared, standing in the doorway.

"Henry Berry," Pollie said, "Rhoda wants to see you."

Henry handed his instrument to the nearest man and sprinted toward the open door. Neither foot touching the front steps. Once inside, Pollie grabbed him by the arm to slow him down and reminded him that Rhoda was still very weak. "Go gently," she advised.

At first, Henry just peeked around the doorframe and knocked on the wood, "Anyone home?" he asked.

Rhoda was in bed, dressed in a white nightgown. Her hair was combed, and she was sitting up. She looked at him and grinned. "You've been a great dad, so far. How are you holding up?" she chided.

Henry walked over and was almost overwhelmed by how pretty she looked. He knelt down beside her bed, put his arms around her, and said, "Did you see Sally Ann? She's the most beautiful little girl in the world. You did just great, Momma. I am so proud of you!"

Rhoda laughed and admitted, "Yeah, Sally Ann is a doll. Thank you, Daddy."

And the two new parents just sat together looking at their new daughter as she slept in the little cradle next to the bed.

CHAPTER 20

Elizabeth walked to the side of the large hearth where a roaring fire kept the December chill at bay. Her move also allowed her to avoid the great cloud of cigar smoke that was collecting and rising from the middle of the room toward the high ceiling.

She addressed the group of men gathered in her house as equals. These were the wealthy men of the area, and together they manipulated the system with their money and connections—the sheriffs, the judges, the elected officials. They had the best representatives in government that money could buy. These people really had the power, because their paid representatives were put there to write laws that benefited their business dealings. Most importantly, they were the ones whose companies would be hired to build the bridges, roads, schools, and hospitals. This was where the money was made. These wealthy landowners felt more than entitled to their high fees because only they had the connections to organize, plan, develop, and deliver the projects that benefited everyone in the state. They were the job-creators.

Elizabeth had always been involved with her husband's business dealings, and he had confided in her often. He knew she had a sharp business mind and a keen sense for making money. It was for this reason that the men gathered here accepted her as her husband's auxiliary, and they listened intently to her words.

She began, "As you are all so painfully aware, our country is an occupied state. The Union Army has sent troops to 'guard our safety' (everyone chuckled at the sarcasm), and they have dismissed our state congress. We have no say in the political affairs of our state, and we will not be readmitted into the U.S. Congress until we ratify the 14th Amendment. In addition, they require us to 'swallow the dog' and pledge our oath of allegiance to the United States of America, its Constitution, and to renounce our state's secession and replace our current state constitution with one that reflects the will of our oppressors.

"Gentlemen, they mean to humiliate us to the core! Even after, we have done what they ask. We, the upper class of society, must write a letter to the U.S. Congress and beg forgiveness in order for our rights to be restored!

"At this time, gentlemen, I am too full of hate and pride to kiss their collective ass."

Mary Norment, who was there with her husband, as always, blushed at the crude terms.

The men responded with shouts of, "Here! Here!"

Elizabeth's words rang out in the big room, "We are the monarchs of this land. It is the ownership of land that gives us our power, connections, privileges, and way of living. The smaller plantations do not know what wealth and power are, so they are now struggling financially. They do not know that real wealth is not acquired, it is *inherited*. We have been bred to lead and manage these lands. Our heritage certifies the status of our social class and demands we be treated better than the lower classes. They were put here to serve us, not the other way around. It is God's intention, and hand, behind our blessings. And, gentlemen, even as we gather to plan for the new world that affronts us, we will remain and rebuild. God truly is on our side, and **the South will rise again!**"

Hearing this, everyone jumped out of their chairs, stood, and applauded Elizabeth's inspirational words.

Someone in the group started singing Dixie and, without missing a beat, the rest of the group joined in for a heartfelt rendition of their beloved song, *their* National Anthem.

At the end of the song, they all yelled, "Hurrah!" and shot back what brandy remained in their snifters before holding their empty glasses high as a gesture of salute and a toast to their way of life as Southern aristocrats.

Everyone in the room returned to their seats feeling energized and refreshed. Maybe the South could still somehow be saved. Their optimism was high, and all their attention focused on Elizabeth, a leader with an idea and a plan.

Elizabeth began to look up into the smoke cloud that had gathered near the ceiling. She gazed into the smoke as if she was looking into a crystal ball. As she began to speak, it was as though she was telling the others what she saw as their reality but in a new light.

"Gentlemen, as much as we hated Lincoln and cheered when Andrew Johnson became President, the truth is he doesn't have the ability to control Congress. I've heard you all speaking about this as we ride the train or meet socially," confided Elizabeth, "and what some of you may not know is that Andrew Johnson is a member of the Free Masons, as was my husband. More importantly, the former Tennessee senator was born and raised in Raleigh and is my third cousin."

This revelation caused a bit of a stir in the group for it meant Elizabeth knew something they did not.

After a pause, Elizabeth's gaze returned from the heavens to address those seated around the room, "Gentlemen, we have the means to obtain and provide financial services at a very profitable margin. There are no banks. So, where are the farmers and merchants to go for financial assistance. No doubt, the local business entrepreneurs would rather borrow from us than from any damned Scalawag or Carpetbagger. Moreover, those that renege on their loans will lose their land, and we will take ownership. This is especially true when we deal with the Indians. Their land has some of the best timber in the area and is close to the rail lines and the river all the way to the coastal ports.

"But our problem is also that we have so much land. Our workforce has been set free. So, how do we obtain the manpower to perform the labor required at a cost that is *most profitable*?

"Gentlemen, when I felt most deeply that God had forsaken us and our cause, I received a revelation that it was not God's intention that we fight with guns and cannons. We are supposed to use our powerful connections to write the laws of the land in our favor. It is the way to control the Republic.

"At present, there are strangers and imposters in our State House and Congress. But they are not politicians and government, law and politics is no place for amateurs. Why, did you know the Radicals have organized the black vote so they can continue to oppress us in the future? Did you know they have elected fifteen blacks to our state congress?" added Elizabeth to stoke her audience.

"What?" someone shouted.

"How can this be?" someone else asked.

Then, the crowd's words became just a loud rumble, and no one was listening. They just said whatever came to mind after that punch to the gut.

"Gentlemen! Gentlemen!" shouted Elizabeth until the group again quieted down. "Let me continue, please.

There will be an election coming up soon, and we must use our time to divide our enemies and unite the white citizens. Major Norment has assured me his Ku Klux Klan will work tirelessly to persuade the blacks it is in their best interest to stay out of politics and not vote. We will win back our government, and we *will* return to our former profitable state."

"But how if we don't have a cheap, reliable labor force?" said a voice from the back of the room, speaking the thought on everyone's mind.

"As I was saying, without Southern representation in the U.S. Congress, every veto President Johnson uses, the Radical Congressmen continue to override. And so it seems, he can do nothing for us. However, my friends, that sly old fox, Johnson, has thrown us a bone."

Elizabeth paused again to gauge the reaction of the group before her. She had their rapt attention.

"We will likely have to bow to those currently in power... and swallow our pride... for a while. We'll just have to accept what punishment the damned Yankees place on us. But it will not last. They, too, are beat-up, tired, and weary from the war. They too, want to move on. The world has changed, and we must change, too. However, this change will be by our own direction, not theirs, and we will win back our government.

"I do understand that the Scalawags up in Raleigh are planning to conduct hearings into the deaths of certain local Indians by the heroes of our former Home Guard, some of the most powerful men in the state," Elizabeth continued. "In fact, some of those prominent men are here with us today." She pointed out O. C. Norment with a wink, a smile and a nod, eliciting laughter from the group. "However," she said, "1 am of the opinion that our state officials will be inclined to do nothing against the accused. This is why we are powerful and the managers of this democracy."

Elizabeth walked over to a writing table in the corner of the room under one of the large windows, opened the center drawer, and pulled out a document. She turned to the crowd and said, "Here is the bone President Johnson has given us." She read the newly enacted Thirteenth Amendment to the group. The Amendment abolishes slavery and involuntary servitude **except** *as punishment for a crime.*

Again, Elizabeth paused, though this time for dramatic effect. "I'll say that last part again because it is the 'bone' Johnson has thrown us. '*Except* **as punishment for a crime**.' Gentlemen, do you realize how many of these freedmen have run off? Where will they work? Most will likely turn to stealing, which is a crime, or they will be homeless. Vagrancy, too, is a crime. Plus, there will be fines to pay. Where *will* these freedmen get the money?

"I've been working closely with Mary and Owen Norment and our lawyers and politicians for an arrangement of what we call the 'Convict Lease Program' that should supply us with all the labor we need at a price we can live with. After all, we don't *need* slavery!

"Here's how we see it working. First, the state can't really afford to house and feed the prisoners. Not to mention, there isn't enough space to keep them all in the current prisons, and building new prisons is not at the top of anybody's list of priorities. Second, these freedmen should work for their keep *just like anyone else*."

The crowd indicated they agreed. *Yes*, these men *should* work for their housing and food as well as pay off any fines. This line of thought brought shouts of, "It's only right!"

"And, if they run away or incur additional fines, they'll need to work longer to pay off those fines, too," Elizabeth said as she continued laying out the new concept. "This convict workforce will be under armed guard at all times to maintain our safety. And, the prisoners will be required to wear leg chains so they can't run away. We will house them and feed them as we did when they were slaves. They will be instructed to call our ladies 'Miss' and all white men, 'Master.' Punishment *will be permitted* to reduce lazy or rude behavior along with additional monetary fines.

"It will cost us no more than it did before; we will house and feed them, and *that* will be their pay.

"I do think that our labor problems will soon be over, along with the problem of the idle nigger. Major Norment will be contacting each of you so that you know what part you can play to ensure we achieve control of the politics and laws in this State. Together, we will *again* be successful, and gentility will return to our lands. Say it with me, gentlemen: *'**THE SOUTH WILL RISE AGAIN'!**'"

1868

*Show me a hero
and I will write you a tragedy.*

F. Scott Fitzgerald

Total documented raids on local Plantations by the Lowrie Gang
in **1868** = **4**

CHAPTER 21

Rhoda was unusually quiet when Henry Berry arrived home. The baby was awake and making happy noises in her crib.

"Rhody, is there a problem, sweetheart?" Henry Berry asked, walking over to where she was sitting.

"Bear, I talked with an agent from the Freedman's Bureau, a Mr. John Sanders, about what all's been happening around these parts since the end of the war. They want you to send a letter to petition the Governor for a pardon so you won't be a wanted man no more," Rhoda said softly as she looked lovingly into his eyes. "They say the time is right because the Radicals are about to take up the cases against the men of the Home Guard for killing our people. They say, since we were not part of the war effort because we were forbidden to take up arms, we were the victims and not perpetrators or instigators of the violence in these parts."

"That sounds good, but why would the Governor help us?" wondered Henry out loud.

"We can go see Hector McLean. He's a lawyer, and he was the one that married us. I think we should seek his counsel," suggested Rhoda.

"Okay," Henry said as he pondered the suggestion, "I'll give it some thought."

"I made an appointment with him for us to meet at his office tomorrow," confessed Rhoda as she continued looking into Henry's eyes. She tried to gauge his reaction to what she was saying.

At first, the realization of her making plans without consulting him snapped his head back. But, the heartfelt warmth within the depths of her eyes just melted his heart. The laughter of Sally Ann in the background stirred protective instincts deep within his soul.

"Sure," he said, "we'll go tomorrow and see what might be done."

Just saying the words, made Henry and Rhoda feel more hopeful about the future and the kind of life they might offer their fledgling family. She wrapped her arms around her husband and kissed him for his gentle manner.

The next day, their lawyer drew up the petition and suggested, "Ya'll should go visit your neighbors as a family, in the middle of the day mind you and apologize to the families you stole from. If you act right and calm them toward peace, instead of scaring them away, they just might sign this petition. The more signatures and support of your neighbors you get, the more likely it will be that the governor grants you your pardon. I suggest you start with our old friend, John McNair, Hmmmm? Best to start with the Manor you've robbed most often, because if you can get old-man McNair to sign your petition, it will be more likely the others will sign it, too."

CHAPTER 22

John McNair was rummaging through assorted items stowed away under the main staircase in his manor house. Whenever he had reason to enter this space, the smell of the dust and dry wood would whisk him back to when he was a small boy and would hide in there during a game of hide-'n-seek.

He was looking for a pair of old riding boots that used to be his favorites. He'd looked everywhere upstairs and down, and his frustration was building. This was the last place he could think of to look for the boots. If they weren't here, they likely were stolen by the Lowrie Gang, who had most recently raided his estate early in the year.

The knock at the front door was unexpected. When he opened the door, he was even more surprised to see a lovely neatly dressed woman holding a baby. "Good afternoon, Mr. McNair. May we come in and talk with you, please?" asked the woman.

The baby put the old man at ease, and his southern hospitality kicked in, and he responded with, "Why certainly, do come in," said McNair, smiling as he noticed the baby was smiling back at him.

As he opened the front door fully, someone else stepped forward who had been unseen, standing to woman's right.   John McNair stepped back, wide-eyed and speechless. The man's audacity took his breath away as the man with the woman and child stepped forward; it was Henry Berry Lowrie!

Henry Berry saw the look on the old man's face. He quickly held up his hands to show he was unarmed. "Mr. McNair, please don't be afraid," he said. "We are not here to rob you."

John McNair was confused and frozen to the spot where he stood.

"First, I'd like to introduce you to my wife, Rhoda, and your newest neighbor, Sally Ann." continued Henry Berry.

"I've come here today, seeking your forgiveness for past actions and any harm we may have caused you. What we did was in desperation, enacted in desperate times. I cannot return what we have taken from you. We cannot change the past. But I am here today to tell you that we will not raid anymore and we ask that you sign our petition to the governor to declare a pardon for me and the others in my group that has been declared outlaws.

We don't want to rob and steal. You know the quality of our woodworking skills. Some of your best furniture we made for you. We have worth, and we wish to earn an honest wage to take care of our families.

"I don't want people coming after me anymore. Sign my petition, please and help me get a pardon granted so we will not have to rob nor raid your stores again. We will make your furniture, and you will pay us a fair price for our labor. We want only peace. Deal?" Henry Berry asked.

John McNair was the first of most all the plantation owners to sign the Lowrie petition for a pardon by the North Carolina Governor.

When the Lowries thought they had enough signatures, they gave the paper to Hector McLean. He was most impressed by the number of names and, he said so. "Why, this is a virtual Who's Who of Top Dogs in this part of the country. Nice job, indeed! I'll have this delivered to the Governor's Office within the week. And, you may rest assured that as soon as I hear anything about your case, I'll come by, personally, and give you the news."

There was a firm handshake between the men and Rhoda gave Mr. McLean a genuine hug of appreciation, which embarrassed him immensely.

At last, the raids would end, and the robberies would stop.

Peace would return to Robeson County.

Although, after the Lowries had left his office, McLean picked up the signed petition again, as if to verify what he thought he saw. Something puzzled him, but whatever it was, he couldn't see it. He studied the signatures and could find nothing. Then, it occurred to him. It wasn't *who* was on the list of names, it was whose names were NOT on the list:

- Elizabeth McRae
- Mary and O. C. Norment
- Sheriff Reuben King

CHAPTER 23

Mary Norment was in such high spirits as the little train pulled to a stop at Argyle Station that she was standing in the doorway, waiting for the train to come to a stop. Just the sight of Argyle Manor caused goosebumps as she looked forward to seeing her best friend.

The carriage ride from the depot to the manor house was pleasant enough, though Mary thought the black driver looked at her like she *owed* him something for the ride. "How rude," she thought. Once she started up the stairs and looked again upon the magnificently impressive door that greeted everyone fortunate enough to be welcomed, she forgot all about the driver.

Mary knocked twice and could hear the sound echoing down the great hall. She listened carefully, and not hearing any footfalls on the hardwood floor, turned the doorknob and let herself in. "Hello?" she started to yell but stopped in mid-word when Elizabeth appeared from the back, near the kitchen.

Mary smiled, waved, repeated her "Hello" as she walked toward the back of the house and wondered what Elizabeth would be doing in the kitchen?

As she neared the kitchen doorway, Elizabeth came out and stomped passed Mary, with daggers in her eyes and clenched fists.

"Oh my, Elizabeth, what could be the matter?" Mary asked in a sincerely concerned tone of voice.

Elizabeth disappeared into the study.

By the time Mary entered the room, Elizabeth was seated cross-legged on the sofa, staring out the window, her arms crossed and tears in her eyes.

"Elizabeth! What on Earth is the matter? Please tell me. Don't cry. Tell me what's wrong, please?" pleaded Mary.

They both sat silent for a while; Mary looking at Elizabeth's eyes and holding her hand. Elizabeth just stared out the window and cried. Finally, she took a deep breath - and biting her lower lip at times, told Mary that her house servants had left to *enjoy their freedom*.

"What am I going to do?" Elizabeth cried out. "This is because of the damned mettlesome Freedman's Bureau!" she shrieked. "Because of them, Edith and Ben are acting like they're 'uppity niggers,' 'land-owners,' and my *business* partners! Why, they even brought home one of the Bureau's agents, who came with written employment contracts in-hand. Said my servants were free to live where they wished. *He said that TO ME!* The insulting, disrespectful little shit. Do you KNOW where they are going to be living? Do you? You remember the Davis Farm that wasn't doing so well? Well, turns out the widow couldn't manage the farm and couldn't pay her taxes, so she just abandoned the property. Do you know what the Freedman's Bureau turned around and DID with that land? They parceled off about forty acres, along with the farmhouse, and GAVE IT as a God-damned BRIBE to entice my loving house servants to desert me. Oh, what am I to do?" asked Elizabeth and her sobs came in renewed waves of despair.

Mary tried comforting Elizabeth with a gentle squeeze of the hand. With her free hand, she stroked Elizabeth's hair and moved some of the strands that had fallen over her eyes.

"Where is the contract? May I read it?" asked Mary.

"Help yourself!" said Elizabeth, angrily, and she threw the wadded-up ball of paper she'd been holding in her fist at Mary.

The paper ball bounced off Mary's shoulder and fell to the floor, where Mary picked it up. She walked over to a window where the light was better for reading. She unraveled the crumpled ball of paper as best she could and carefully read the contract.

"Elizabeth, it's not *that* bad, sweetheart. They haven't abandoned you," said Mary softly.

"The hell they haven't!" returned Elizabeth, fire in her eyes. "They left this morning! The goddamned ingrates! Piss on them. I'll get others. Better, too."

"What is today?" Mary asked Elizabeth.

Elizabeth drew her head back a ways, to bring Mary's image into better focus. She narrowed her eyes and wanted to know why the *day* was important?

"Well," Mary said, "According to the contract, they are required to work under your management to perform those duties that are expected of their years of experience, as your house servants. They will arrive here at your house within one hour after sunrise and will be dismissed for the evening at one hour before sunset. Except on special occasions when they might be asked to stay later, in which you would be expected to compensate them for their work, meaning that you will pay them for their overtime. And *today is Sunday*! Their contract states they will work Monday through Saturday, at the aforementioned times, which means that *today* is their day off. They will be BACK TOMORROW MORNING. They did NOT abandon you, and you will not be left alone. This is just another 'adjustment' the Radicals, and damn Yankees are using to bust our grits," explained Mary.

Elizabeth looked all teary-eyed into Mary's face. Mary smiled, and Elizabeth said softly, "Really? They're coming back?"

"Yes, tomorrow," stated Mary firmly.

This visit had certainly not started off as Mary had expected. Oh, well, she thought, I might as well make her day. Mary drew in a deep breath and began, "Elizabeth, we got news that the governor has gotten enough votes to ratify the Fourteenth Amendment, and North Carolina will be readmitted into Union. Now, we'll have a chance to argue for our own cause in Congress."

Elizabeth was all cried out. She just looked numbed by too much information. All she could weakly say was, "Well, I guess it had to happen."

"One more thing," Mary continued, "We, the landowners and more well off, have to beg, in-person, before Congress and grovel for forgiveness and pledge allegiance to the United States of America," Mary said flatly, not knowing what kind of reaction she'd get from Elizabeth.

"I'll eat the dog before I'll bow before them and give them the pleasure of seeing me beg for social status in *their* country! As a white woman, I don't even *have* a vote – and the black man does! Well, *damn them all* - I don't *need* any damned VOTE, because I BUY the influence I need," Elizabeth said through gritted teeth and narrowed eyes, emphasizing her contempt by slamming her fist on the table!

At times, she scared Mary by her actions and wild-eyed facial expressions. "They can all be *God-Damned* before I prostrate myself to any Yankee! No way. The blacks may be called *citizens* with the right to vote, but those damned niggers don't deserve to be *equal* citizens! The sons of bitches will never be *MY equal*, I can tell you that!" concluded Elizabeth.

Mary walked back over to where Elizabeth was seated, sat down, and physically turned Elizabeth to face her. She took both of Elizabeth's hands in her own. Elizabeth looked up into Mary's eyes, though her lips were still pouting.

"Elizabeth, I want to ask you to reconsider your plea to the governor to declare Henry Berry Lowrie, an outlaw. Maybe it's time we put the past behind us?"

Elizabeth's eyes again narrowed, and she almost hissed at Mary, "*Nothing* moves forward for me until I see the killer of my beloved Neal hang!"

Mary let the tension hang in the air for a moment, hoping to allow it dissipate somewhat.

"I understand, <u>and</u> I'm sorry," Mary assured.

"You can *never understand* the assault to my heart, to my life that Henry Berry Lowrie caused me," she cried.

Finally, Mary said, "Elizabeth, I'm sorry I asked. As a Christian, I thought it only right. By the way, today Owen got word that the governor has granted your appeal to keep the $300 reward posted for the outlaw Henry Berry Lowrie: Dead or Alive!"

"Really?", said Elizabeth, looking up at Mary through tear-streaked eyes, trying to comprehend what her friend had just told her.

Then, Elizabeth jumped up. Mary jumped up. They both jumped around in circles as they held hands and laughed and celebrated the first really good news to come down the pike in some time.

"Bless the Lord," laughed Elizabeth. "Our prayers have been answered!"

Then Elizabeth stopped jumping and indicated Mary should stop, too, and look at her.

"Mary," said Elizabeth, "I have some good news to share with you, too. Late yesterday evening, I received word that the state prosecutor has declared *Nolle Prosequi* for each indictment against our heroes from the Home Guard accused of killing those damned Indians."

Mary smiled genuinely and was pleased with the news. Or, at least *thought* she ought to be. Finally, she had to ask, "What does that mean, 'No lay Prosakwee'?"

Elizabeth got a good laugh at Mary's expense because of her mispronunciation of the Latin phrase. "It means the State chooses *not* to prosecute; there is not enough evidence to try the Home Guard. Our men are free and clear!"

To this news, the women hugged each other and did another happy dance. Finally, the day's visit was beginning to improve.

CHAPTER 24

During the spring, the Freedman's Bureau, with the help of their new agent, a former Boston cop named John Sanders, worked closely with the black communities and with the newly elected representatives of the state legislature.

Now was the time for the new citizens to play a part in the democratic process by which they were to be governed. This was their duty as freed blacks. John Sanders worked many long nights writing, editing, and arguing with the black councilmen until they felt they had perfected the wording of what they called their *Declaration of Freedom.* The government would assure:

- The right of every man to vote in all elections.

- Non-whites would have the same right as a white man to admit testimony in court proceedings.

- The right of non-whites to serve on juries equal to whites.

Most of all, the letter expressed their desire for peace, democracy, and that all races be treated equally.

That fall, when the Declaration of Freedom was actually brought to the floor of the state legislature, the documents were duly noted then promptly ignored.

CHAPTER 25

John Sanders indeed seemed to be a man on a mission. He worked long hours with the community leaders to find employment for the new freedmen and saw to it that they obtained any clothes or medicines they needed.

He saw to it that the poor received food. That task was made more difficult by the fact that the surrounding Conservative landowners controlled distribution and transport of all goods. It wasn't unusual for *interruptions of service* to occur with no reasons given.

In time, the Indians and freed blacks became so comfortable with Mr. Sanders, they asked for his advice and guidance. They believed that perhaps he could help remove the *outlaw* status the governor had again placed on Henry Berry Lowrie's head. After all, so many of the poor in Robeson County owed their very lives to this brave man and his band of brothers.

Henry Berry, however, was not a man who trusted outsiders; particularly white men. Fortunately, John Sander's easy-going manner and willingness to openly discuss all aspects of any issue without bias quickly put Henry Berry at ease.

It took several meetings with John Sanders before Henry Berry felt trusting enough to tell him their version of the history behind their story. To which John Sanders simply replied, "I understand. It was a time of war."

Sanders went back to Lumberton and even traveled to Charlotte and Wilmington to talk with lawyers and legal scholars who could provide the best advice about Henry's dilemma. Henry Berry's first petition to the governor had been declined.

When Sanders returned, he immediately sent out word that he needed to talk with Henry Berry as soon as possible. The Indian's grapevine communication system worked its magic, and by that afternoon, John Sanders was seated across from Henry Berry and Rhoda.

"Henry Berry, everyone I talked with has basically advised the same course of action. Their consensus is that you should give yourself up to the new Radical Yankee-controlled government and plead your case before a judge. They all agree that any crimes you may have committed were done so as acts of war during a time of war. You and your people were under great duress, and your lives were at risk. Therefore, it's believed you will be acquitted by the courts, which will remove all bounties on your head." Here, Sanders paused to give the Lowries time to consider what he had just told them. "I do believe this is the only way you and your family will ever be able to live your lives freely and unmolested by sheriffs and bounty hunters."

John Sanders had come to know Henry Berry was not a man to submit to ridicule and humiliation. So, he added, "I've worked a deal with the local officials who have promised you will not be kept in an upper floor cell, but kept on the lower floors of the building where the debtors' prison is located. Additionally, I've been promised that you will not be put in irons, shackled or chained, either in jail or in transport. And, you will receive not two meals a day but three, prepared outside the jailhouse." Sanders then stopped talking as he waited to see Henry Berry's reaction.

Henry Berry looked to Rhoda. "Well, what do you think? Should we take the offer?" he asked.

Rhoda's eyes fixed on her husband's as she repeated the gist of what Sanders had said, "Let's see...you are promised no one will harass or embarrass you. You are promised you will not be submitted to any humiliation, and your case will be allowed to proceed through the legal system in a gentlemanly manner. Lastly, he says your safety would be guaranteed." Her eyes moved to Sander's so she could gauge his demeanor. "Are you *sure* these promises will be kept?" she asked Sanders.

Sanders stated flatly, and convincingly, that there should be no concerns about the agreement or safety. All promises would be kept.

Rhoda looked to Henry and almost whispered, "I'm thinking this is about as good a chance as we'll ever get for justice to be served, a last chance for us to be free. " Henry Berry lowered his head and accepted the offered conditions. Two days later, he surrendered to the military authorities in Wilmington.

John Sanders was at his side every step of the way. There were no problems and Henry Berry was made as comfortable as could be expected. Most of his solitary time was spent thinking about what needed to be said to convince the court to acquit him of outlawing.

When he was not alone, Sanders was usually with him, helping him in every way he could. Within a week, the local Conservative whites learned of the special treatment given to Lowrie. They felt that it was not right or proper for a low-class murdering Indian to be given special privileges when a white man was in shackles for stealing a horse!

Over the next couple of days, it seemed that more and more objects were being hurled at the window over Henry Berry's cell. The shouted epithets grew louder as each new group grew in size. Henry Berry Lowrie wasn't so sure his safety *could* be guaranteed, not against a mob hell-bent on a hanging!

This was brought up that evening when John Sanders came by after dinner. He was concerned, too. He promised Henry Berry that he would take it up with administrative officials to ensure his safety.

Later that evening, yet another, drunker crowd of men came to the jailhouse to demand that Henry be released and subjected to their demands.

Lowrie became very apprehensive when the deputy came down to unlock his cell. "You'll have to come with me," the deputy said. "The sheriff says we need to move you to the second floor. It's for your own safety."

Henry protested and said it wasn't part of the deal and if they weren't going to keep the deal they'd all agreed to, what the hell was the point of moving upstairs? They had promised him he would not be held in the jail upstairs.

When they got to the top of the stairs, there was a set of irons and shackles lying on the bench beside the entrance door to the second-floor jail cells. "What are those irons for?" asked Henry Berry.

"Well, I'm going to have to put them on you once you're in the cell. You see, the sheriff thinks if the crowd knows you're not being treated better than a white man, they'll likely leave. It's for your own protection," repeated the deputy, as he used his right hand to unlock the large door bolt and his left hand to grab the door and swing it open.

As he stepped back to allow Henry Berry to enter, he saw that Henry Berry was holding a Navy Colt Revolver and it was pointed at the deputy's midsection. The deputy reacted by quickly dropping his hand to his side and found his holster empty.

"That's a pretty slick trick, son. But now what do you intend to do," asked the deputy as the taste of bile crept up his throat.

Henry Berry told the deputy to relock the door and then motioned him to move back downstairs. They went back to the cell where Henry had been held, and the deputy was told to go inside. Henry then locked the door.

"Eustis," said Henry Berry to the deputy, "You know I know where you and your wife live. I don't want a feud with you but if you call out or set off an alarm within the next fifteen minutes, you better run far from this county because I will find you. Do we have an understanding, here?"

"Yes, sir, Mr. Lowrie. No problem. I won't make a sound," stuttered the deputy as he realized he was screwed. Either he'd get killed by the sheriff for letting Lowrie escape or Lowrie would kill him, for real. The deputy quickly added, "I wish you much luck, Mr. Lowrie!"

Henry Berry left the jail and walked out into the night and mingled among the men and shouted a few insults at the jailhouse himself, before disappearing into the night on his way home to his family.

1869

*True courage is not
the brutal force of vulgar heroes,
but the firm resolve
of virtue and reason.*

Alfred North Whitehead

Total documented raids on local plantations by the Lowrie Gang
in **1869** = **3**

CHAPTER 26

The talk in The Settlement was all about the news that the military had conducted a survey and found that in the past year, 1868, the Ku Klux had killed twenty-three blacks and whipped or flogged more than 200 men and women. And, that was just in North Carolina.

Still, the white conservatives were flabbergasted, livid that black men, men who had been their livestock just months before, were now elected officials in public office. Damn Yankees! They should stay out of the South's business!

What was being forced on Southern white men was just wrong. Worse, blacks were now challenging the whites for jobs! What would be next? Would they want the white women, too? God damn! All this was the black's fault, of course, and they would not get away with it. The Ku Klux would see to that.

Deep in the swamp the woods were so thick a man could hide ten feet away and you would never see him. This was a place the Klan was not familiar with and did not enter. The Indians could have the swamp for all they cared, which was why Tom Lowrie was surprised to see white men surveying his land.

He didn't recognize the men, so he approached them in a friendly manner and played the dumb Indian, asking all kinds of questions. The survey team said they were from Charlotte and had been hired by a Mr. Rueben King. They'd heard he was the sheriff somewhere in this area. It was on his commission that the men were surveying the land and dense forest. Sheriff King needed the land survey in order for him to file his deed for the land.

"Who owns this land and how much did the sheriff pay for it?" Tom inquired.

"That's not part of our business or our concern. We don't know the answer to those questions. We can only tell you where the boundary lines are running," the foreman replied. "Day after tomorrow you may be able to get that information at the courthouse. That's where the land deeds will need to be registered and properly titled."

CHAPTER 27

The sun had set and night shadows were covering the trees and underbrush when the carriage pulled up in front of the two-story brick house with big white columns adorning the front porch.

The driver called for his stableman to take the carriage up to the barn, rub the horse down, and put him to bed.

As he walked toward the front door of his manor home, Rueben King realized he was exhausted, dead tired. Life was becoming too stressful. He'd lost his bid for reelection. He was tired of living alone. Business was no fun anymore.

He stopped in mid-stride and looked up absentmindedly to inspect the manor's slate roof, but the light had faded. So he just ambled up the front stairs, crossed the front porch and swung open the front door. The foyer to his home was large with hardwood floors. Wearily, he shuffled his feet toward the far end of the hall and the parlor. His leather-soled boots shushed across the floor as they scratched deeper gouges into the wood.

As he walked toward the fireplace, he was startled when a match was struck to light a hurricane lantern on a nearby table. The sheriff was a big man, and he wasn't intimidated easily. When his eyes adjusted to the light, he recognized the man who'd lit the lantern. It was Henry Berry Lowrie, sitting in his parlor like he lived there.

For a moment, neither man said a word. Both just observed the other. King didn't look like he was armed. Henry Berry was wearing a Colt Navy Revolver on each hip and had twin bandoliers across his chest. The handle of a Bowie knife could be seen across his belt buckle.

"What are you doing in my house?" the Sheriff finally demanded.

"I've come for the deeds to our land and your gold," said Henry Berry, matter-of-factly.

"What makes you think I have the deeds to your land?" demanded the Sheriff.

"Don't play games, Rueben. I mean to get those documents and to steal all the gold you have in your safe," stated Henry as he stared at Sheriff King.

Neither man blinked.

King walked over to the fireplace, moved the screen over to the side, and threw a couple of logs onto the iron grates. He picked up some paper lying on top of a desk, balled it up and placed it under the logs. He struck a match and lit the paper. Rueben King watched the flames climb up and over the wood. Henry Berry watched Rueben King.

"I must say," said King, "you're mighty stupid to come here."

Henry just watched and listened as the sheriff busied himself and appeared to be minding the fire, sort of absentmindedly, like he was considering something.

"What makes you think, if I had the deeds, I'd give them to you?" intoned Rueben King.

"Because I'll kill you if I have to," was Henry Berry's reply.

The sheriff seemed to ponder the thought as he replaced the metal fire poker into its stand by the fireplace.

"Maybe we can work something out," suggested the Sheriff. "Look in the table beside you and you'll find the papers you're after."

Henry turned and opened the drawer. Inside there were papers. Henry Berry had never been taught to read or attend school, by law, so he couldn't tell if the papers were the deeds to his land, or not. He pulled the papers out and looked at them to see if they *looked* like deeds. He'd seen deeds before, and these didn't look right to him. As he studied the papers, his peripheral vision caught the Sheriffs right hand rise up to reach inside his coat. He pulled out a small handgun and pointed it at Henry's chest.

"I ought to arrest you for entering my home. Instead, I think I'll kill you for breaking and entering," hissed Rueben King. "You've made your last mistake, boy."

Henry Berry just looked at him like he was bored. It was as if there was no threat and he made no effort to move as the enraged Sheriff King aimed the pistol between Henry's eyes. Blood erupted on the front of his shirt and across Henry Berry's face.

Sheriff Rueben King fell face-first onto the granite mantel of the fireplace. He'd dropped the gun, and his right hand was lying over the logs. The flames danced around his fingers. A thick stream of blood pooled beneath his chest and began to spread across the floor.

George Applewhite stepped out from the shadows, white smoke still wafting from the end of his gun. He just nodded at Henry who returned the gesture. Then he walked out of the room to cover the front door, reloading his weapon as he left.

Henry took out his bandanna and wiped the blood off his face. Then he searched the sheriff's pockets and took all the papers he could find.

Tom Lowrie rushed in, saw the sheriff, and said nothing.

"You and Steven ransack the house and gather up any important looking papers, deeds, gold or silver you can find," ordered Henry Berry. "I'm going to go watch the entrance road."

CHAPTER 28

As the last rays of the setting sun illuminated the trees surrounding their land, Edith came out to tell her husband that dinner was ready. But her husband, Ben, asked if she would just sit with him on the front porch of their house and watch the sunset.

In the fading light, Edith could see the sweat running down the side of Ben's cheeks taking the garden dirt with it and leaving little rivers of clean skin mapping the man's dusty face. The couple sat down, and Ben put his arm around Edith's shoulders. She laid her head on his arm.

"My dear," said Ben, softly, "I think we'll have a really good harvest in a few weeks. I suspect there will be more than enough to get us through the winter. Next spring, if we have any of your canned goods left, maybe we can make some extra money with them. Would that be agreeable to you?"

Edith wasn't really listening. She was lost in her own thoughts, trying to get the most out of this wondrous moment. They were not only free; they were buying their own home and land. They had steady employment at Argyle. The Progressives (Radicals, to the Conservative whites) had control of the government and there were even black men elected to office. Life was so full of hope and promise that Edith almost burst into song!

"Ben," she said, "tomorrow is Sunday, our day off. Let's, for once, sleep in late just because we can. Would you like that as much as I would?"

Ben just laughed. The thought caught him off guard. Sleeping late was never tolerated when he was enslaved and now that he realized he was truly FREE what better way to enjoy one's freedom than to sleep late on your day off?

"I bet I can sleep later than you can," Ben prodded his loving wife.

"Betcha can't!" laughed Edith.

The darkness began to seem dangerous, somehow. But, the smell of hot soup and baked bread was too appealing to be denied. Both Edith and Ben got up a little stiffer than they expected, causing another chuckle between them as they saw each other's signs of getting older. They were free, and they were happy. They were truly blessed and their prayers before dinner expressed their appreciation for all that God had given them in his infinite grace.

Their dinner that night was the best they'd ever eaten. Not because the food was so plentiful but because it was *their food* enjoyed in *their home*. Each time one happened to catch the other's eye was a cause to break out with a big grin. Nothing more needed to be said. They both were living in the moment together and they couldn't have felt closer. They finally understood: *they were* **free!**

There wasn't a lot of conversation during dinner. The two were content to enjoy the food and fall away into their own private thoughts. After the table was cleared, Edith put the dishes in her washtub and dumped in a bucket of water. She hummed a little song she'd learned in church and happily went about her chores.

Ben was on the back porch sitting in a rainwater-filled wooden barrel that was the other half of the barrel Edith was using as a washtub. This was the family bathtub and the pace at which Ben had worked in the waning sunshine to finish hoeing their garden had left him smelling of sweat. Once he'd had the chance to soap-up and rinse off, he began to feel human again. It was nice to feel so clean and fresh. For some reason, the sensation made him think about how much he loved his wife.

Out of the tub, standing on his back porch naked while drying himself with a towel, he heard the thunder of horses coming down the lane toward his house. He quickly put on a clean set of trousers, yelled inside to Edith that someone was coming, and grabbed his shirt before walking around to the front of his house to greet the riders.

Ben put on his shirt but didn't have time to button it up before the group of hooded-riders was upon him. Terrified, he tried to ask about the reason for their visit, but his request was cut short by a kick in the face by the first hooded-rider closest to him, knocking him to the ground.

Other riders surrounded his house. Each rider carried a torch and they wore burlap bags over their heads with eye-holes and jagged stitching that made terrifying masks of evil and hate.

Edith, seeing Ben lying on the ground with blood on his face, swung open the front door and started to run to her fallen husband. Instead, she was knocked back into her house by the shock of a rifle stock to her forehead that knocked her unconscious before she hit the floor.

Several of the hooded men dismounted and roughly picked Ben up off the ground and immediately bound his hands and feet with rope.

"What do you want?" Ben screamed. "We haven't done anything to you! Who are you? What do you want?"

Everyone seemed to be yelling at once—hate-spewed words from the hooded horsemen and panicked shrieks of fear from Ben.

"I haven't done anything! What do you want?" Ben kept yelling.

From what Ben could make out, they were angry with him that he knew how to read and was working with the Freedman's Bureau to teach other blacks how to read. They screamed at him that he was such an uppity nigger that he thought he could run for political office now that the God damn blacks could vote like they were equal to white men. How dare he!

What was needed was to make an example of freed blacks that try to act uppity in a white society. As one of the men threw a rope over a big branch of a nearby oak tree, others rode around the house tossing their torches through windows and into the open doors.

As the flames grew angrier inside the house, Ben was hoisted off the ground by the rope around his neck. As the pressure in his skull grew and his legs kicked under him, he swung around and could see inside his burning house. On the floor, he saw Edith start to move and make her way toward the back door as flames began to shoot from the windows and roof rafters. Ben tried to call out to Edith, but the rope cut into his voice box, and his eyes failed him. Soon he was dead.

CHAPTER 29

Elizabeth was startled from a restless sleep by a frantic pounding on the massive front door of Argyle, causing her to bolt upright, quickly lifting her out of bed and onto her feet, wide-eyed with terror.

BOOM! BOOM! BOOM! Came the frantic pounding of fists upon the double doors setting off frightening echoes through the spacious foyer and throughout the once quiet house. Elizabeth quickly put on her night robe, grabbed her loaded double-barreled shotgun, and rushed to the stairway.

"Who's there?!" yelled Elizabeth from the top of the stairs.

The knocking on the door stopped and the echoes faded from the house.

"Who's there?!" Elizabeth yelled once more.

Someone on the other side of the door was saying something, but what could not be understood. Elizabeth came to realize that it was a woman's voice and that she was crying, hysterically.

Elizabeth ran down the stairs, across the broad hallway, unlocked the front doors, and swung them open to find a black woman curled up with her face buried in her folded arms. She was crying so hard she could barely catch her breath. The woman looked up at Elizabeth, and she tried to say something but was overcome with grief. A torrent of tears flowed over her cheeks and blood was streaming down her face from a gash that ran over the bridge of her nose, through her right eyebrow and across her forehead.

In the faint morning light, Elizabeth was stunned to recognize this wretched soul as her beloved house servant, Edith.

"Edith!" screamed Elizabeth. "What has happened? Where is Ben?"

Elizabeth helped Edith to her feet, took her inside the house to the nearest couch, and sat her down. Elizabeth then ran off to the kitchen, grabbed a couple of towels, and quickly thrust one into the bucket of water in the sink. She grabbed a cup and filled it from the bucket and then ran back to Edith. She handed Edith the cup of water and told her to drink.

Elizabeth then found the hurricane lamp on the table by the window and set it alight. She then took the wet towel and wiped the blood away from Edith's eyes, dabbing gently at the wound across her face.

Edith just sat on the sofa, exhausted from the terror, the trauma, the endurance run to Argyle. She was all cried out. She felt like an empty shell and looked off into the horizon as Elizabeth treated her wounds.

"Tell me what happened," said Elizabeth softly, as she continued to apply pressure to the gash across Edith's face.

For a moment, Edith couldn't respond.

Finally, she looked up into Elizabeth's eyes and blurted out, "They done hanged Ben! Miss Betsy, they killed him and burned our home!" She buried her bloody face in Elizabeth's breasts and again began to cry her heart out. Snot ran down her chin and mixed with the blood and tears as she cried out in confusion. "Why would they hurt Ben? He was such a good kind man. They killed him *for what?!*"

In the morning light, the two women sat crying together. Time stood still. Elizabeth's tears fell hard as she recalled the night, she sat holding her own dying husband.

1870

Our heroes are those... who...

act above and beyond the call of duty

and in so doing

give definition to patriotism

and elevate all of us....

America is the land of the free

because we are the home

of the brave.

David Mahoney

Total documented raids on local plantations by the Lowrie Gang
in **1870 = 8**

CHAPTER 30

Early in 1870, the Progressive (Radical-controlled) U.S. Congress passed the Fifteenth Amendment to the Constitution over President Johnson's veto. The new law stated that no citizen can be denied the right to vote on the basis of race.

The new law meant that blacks and Indians, alike, felt empowered by their new political standing. The Progressives wanted the new voters to participate in the running of the state and the country. They understood that their voices were needed in Raleigh and in Washington to further the Reconstruction efforts and fully integrate the former Confederate State. These freedmen were eager to be a part of this renewed country. They sought for everyone to realize the rights and equalities of all classes. Their shout was *Let freedom ring!*

Each office open for elected officials had six to ten people running as viable candidates. Few had any real financial backing or experience, but they were empowered and enthused by the encouragement and support of their family and friends. Everyone was excited about the future.

The Conservative whites, on the other hand, included ONLY whites. Their platform included ideas such as:

- No welfare for the poor
- No minimum wage for workers
- No workers' unions
- Reduced taxes on the wealthy
- No taxation on tobacco or cotton
- No regulation of private property

- Elimination of government controls on trade
- Abolishment of all regulation on banks
- Unrestricted free business markets
- Encouragement of private citizens and groups to fight crime
- No U.S. intervention in the conflicts of other countries
- No mixing between the social classes (races), "not Equal and Separate"
- Governments should stay out of education
- End to Reconstruction and the removal of all Union troops

When the election results were published, the Radicals had split their votes, allowing the white Conservatives to regain their political power.

CHAPTER 31

"**W**ould you care for more brandy, Major Norment?" asked Edith as she leaned over with a tray carrying a bottle of brandy.

"Why, yes, I think would," drawled Owen Clinton Norment in his best Southern accent.

He smiled and focused on his glass so as not to stare at the bloody scab across Edith's face. When Mary and O. C. Norment arrived at Argyle, they had been shocked and dismayed by Elizabeth's story of finding poor Edith at her doorstep. How cowardly and cruel they all agreed and offered Edith their most sincere sympathies.

Now though, as the brandy started to kick-in among the group gathered at Argyle, their victory celebration began in earnest.

"That should show those damned Progressives, Scalawags, and Carpetbaggers a thing or two about politics! We have kicked their asses! And, we have regained control of our state government by electing true Conservatives to represent our cause. Why we even put six of our seven delegates back into the U.S. Congress. We have done well, my friends," offered Elizabeth. "A toast to our first major victory since the war and the start of many more!" The group of wealthy businessmen, landowners, and their wives all held their glasses high and shouted, "The South will rise again. Hip-hip-hurray!"

"Now we can have our government reestablish some social order in these here parts. We can put those damned darkies back in their place where they belong. You know they are not ready for full citizenship. Hell, most don't want to work; yet they want to be our equals. Dream on is what I say! The future is ours," slurred

Elizabeth, who was gleeful for several reasons. The most important was that she'd solved her labor problems and Argyle was again becoming most productive. As she had said, President Johnson had thrown them a bone by his wording of the Thirteenth Amendment to the United States Constitution. Although it did abolish slavery and involuntary servitude, it included the wording, *except as punishment for a crime*. And, there were an awful lot of blacks disappearing and put in jail for most any "crime." These criminals were punished by being leased to work in the fields of the very plantations they'd been freed from as slaves. Now, they were back doing the same work, with no pay, as members of chain gangs, bossed around by shotgun-toting white supervisors.

These poor blacks were now being treated worse than when they were slaves. Now, if a man died in the field, the owner did not lose any money on his investment in labor. A new convict was simply brought out to replace the dead one.

The wealthy landowners, with the right connections, now had all the manual labor they needed at a cost LESS than what they had been paying before the war. Evidently, the South was in God's good graces again.

As the afternoon light faded, the inebriated group felt inspired. O. C. Norment offered a prayer to thank God for his merciful blessings. Everyone left the party happy.

Elizabeth was feeling a little tipsy but elated at how well her first party since the war had gone. She was smiling all the way to the top of the stairs until she caught sight of her bedroom and the window where Neil had died. Then her smile faded, and she ran to throw herself onto her bed and cry herself to sleep.

Downstairs, Edith cleaned up the mess before she retired to her lonely little room behind the kitchen. She, too, cried herself to sleep, thinking about Ben and how much she missed him.

CHAPTER 32

Word came to Henry Berry that the Ku Klux Klan was gathering in Maxtown, where they had been drinking most of the day. It was said they were there because they were going out again that night to "teach some niggers a lesson."

The group of armed men in Maxtown waited till dark. Every other man carried a torch, and every man wore a menacing looking burlap bag as a hood to hide his identity. As the group rode off into the night, the last man in line had come late to the party and followed a short distance behind the other riders. This man was Henry Berry Lowrie. He wanted to see, firsthand, what the group was up to.

The horsemen numbered about fifty and were strung out single file for almost a quarter mile. After about an hour's ride, Henry Berry could hear gunshots, shouts and saw the glow of fire above the trees before he arrived at the scene.

As he rode around a bend in the road, he saw a farmhouse and barn ablaze. Most of the men were walking about drinking, yelling, shooting off handguns. Two black men hung from a nearby tree.

One of the Klan members got too close to someone's torch, and his hood caught fire. His drunken friends pulled the hood off before the man's hair could catch on fire. The light from the house fire lit up the man's face, who was standing not more than five feet away from Henry Berry and Henry realized he recognized the man. He just couldn't place where he'd seen him. He didn't know his name. But his FACE stirred Henry's soul and told him the man was "special."

The feeling was puzzling to Henry Berry, but long ago he'd learned to trust his inner voice. He backed away into the shadows and moved away from the group so that he could follow this man and find out where he lived.

After the men had caused as much chaos and destruction of the property as possible, or at least until they got bored, they all ambled off the way they had come, single file. In turn, man after man said their "good night," waved to the group and moved off toward their own homes and family.

Eventually, the man Henry had recognized waved his own "good night" and took a fork in the road. Henry allowed himself to be passed by the last of the trailing riders. Then, he disappeared back into the shadows, pulled the hood off his head, and also took the same fork in the road, keeping his target in sight.

As they approached the main gate to a manor house, Henry Berry could make out the large white house. Its grand white columns extending from the first-floor porch all the way past the third-floor porch to support the roof.

Henry Berry left his horse tied up in the woods and crept closer to the barn where the man was putting away his horse's saddle and rubbing the animal down to ensure it was dry before retiring.

When his chore was finished, the man took the lantern from where it was hanging on a nearby post. He walked outside and shut the barn doors. For a final check, the man lifted his lantern to shoulder height so he could see that the door's bolt was secured. Satisfied, he picked up his rifle in his free hand and walked away.

From where Henry Berry was standing in the shadows, he had a chance to study the man's face. Why did he recognize this man? How did he come to know this man's face?

Across the lawn and up the front stairs, the man wearily made his way to the front door of his Antebellum-style home.

For Henry Berry, the recall and significance of the man in front of him took his breath away. *THIS* was the man who'd been sitting in the carriage and gave the orders to Brantley Harris to murder his father and brother!

The man closed the front door behind him and didn't notice Henry Berry walking toward the house.

As the man was about to walk upstairs, there was a knock on his front door. He paused, sighed, and walked back to see who was at his door at such an hour, thinking it one of his Ku Klux brothers. He opened the door and held the lantern out to illuminate the front porch. No one was standing on the porch, so he opened the door wider until he saw a man standing at the bottom of the front steps. The night's skies had a break in the clouds, and the moonlight was so bright the shadow under Henry's hat covered his face like a mask.

"Who is it, and what do you want," the agitated man asked, bluntly.

"I'm Henry Berry Lowrie, and I'm here to kill you for ordering the murder of my father and brother," Henry stated, matter-of-factly.

The man turned white as a sheet, pulled himself back inside the house, and quickly closed the door behind him. Through the windows that framed the front door, Henry could see the man blowout the lantern and then heard the man's back slam against the front door, forming a blockade against intrusion. Henry fired both barrels of his shotgun into the middle of the door and heard the man on the other side moan and hit the hardwood floor.

CHAPTER 33

Mary was awakened by her husband's heavy footsteps on the foyer's hardwood floor. When she heard the knock on their front door, she was curious to see who was there. She went to the window overlooking the front yard and could see a man back away from the front porch. She heard her husband call out and clearly heard the man say he was Henry Berry Lowrie. Then there was an explosion, and she heard herself scream as she ran toward the staircase. She came down the stairs as fast as her panic could move her. She got to the bottom of the spiral staircase, and as she turned toward the front door, she stepped onto the blood-spattered foyer and fell down hard, almost knocking her out. But the adrenalin racing through her veins didn't allow any physical pain to register as she clawed her way toward where her husband had fallen.

She slipped and slid her way to Owen and tried to pick him up and cradle him in her arms. His weight was too much for her, and they both fell against the wall and slid down to the floor. Owen was still warm and, his blood continued to pool across the floor when Mary became aware of something sliding down her arm - and pulsating. She lifted her arm so that the moonlight illuminated it and saw there was a piece of heart muscle that beat one last time.

The realization of the horror around her brought bile up from her stomach, seeming as if the evil moment had materialized and grabbed her by the throat, choking her. At the same time, she heard the most horrific soul-wrenching screams of agony that seemed to surround her from within. She broke away from the blood-soaked body and clawed for the door. She had to get out. She had to get help. She had to get away from the screaming!

Dressed only in her nighty, covered in blood and screaming, shouting bloody murder, she ran toward the small train station that connected Norment Manor to Argyle.

Mr. Townsend, the train's engineer, lived beside the depot with his wife. Their daughter had died of the Yellow Jack more than five years ago, and their only son killed at Fort Fisher. Both people were light sleepers and the shots had startled them awake. When all was quiet, they didn't give the sounds much thought and were about to go back to sleep when they heard Mary Norment's screams.

By the time Mary was seen running toward the station, Townsend was dressed and running to meet her. When they met, she flung herself into his arms and cried out, "He's dead! He's dead! Oh my God, he's shot dead!" She just kept crying and crying out, "He's shot dead!"

Mrs. Townsend quickly came out, still dressed in her robe, and tried to get Mary to come inside her house. She needed to get the blood washed off Mary because every time Mary noticed the red slime, she'd begin screaming hysterically.

Finally, they managed to bring Mary into the house, and Mr. Townsend ran to Norment Manor and found the remains of O. C. Norment. The engineer ran back to the depot and started sending signals across the telegraph to Argyle Station. It took a while before old Robert was awakened by the clatter of incoming signals, waiting for him to confirm he was ready to take a message. Robert held his breath as his sleep-filled mind tried to comprehend the words:

OWEN SHOT DEAD

STOP

COME QUICK

STOP

CHAPTER 34

The morning light gave way to a bright, cloudless, blue sky that acted as a backdrop to the billowing smoke and steam from the little Argyle train as it raced toward Norment Manor. Inside her carriage car, Elizabeth sat silently staring out the window looking into nothingness. She still held the telegram crumpled in her fist.

Occasionally, she'd look at the words on the paper to see if perhaps she had not read the brief message correctly, or the message had miraculously changed, or she was having a nightmare and would be jolted awake. Instead, she tried to empathize with her best friend but found she could not feel anything. She was overwhelmed by so many feelings that she seemed to have sunk into a catatonic state, frozen between thoughts and unable to move.

When the train's whistle announced its arrival at Norment Manor, the steam whistle's scream brought Elizabeth back to Earth as a woman on a mission. She was focused on getting done what needed to be done and getting her best friend back to Argyle as quickly as possible.

Before the train had entirely stopped, Mr. Townsend was helping Elizabeth off the train and telling her what he knew about what had happened, which was not much. He was awakened by the sound of gunshots and, shortly thereafter, he heard Mary's cries for help and they'd taken her in. Then he'd sent the telegram to Argyle.

Elizabeth did not ask to see the body of O. C. Norment, nor did she even want to set foot in the house. Instead, she gave orders to have the body sent to the undertakers, and the house cleaned and purged of all signs of the incident.

Mary, who was now wrapped in a blanket, was half-carried to her seat on the train by Elizabeth and Mrs. Townsend. Elizabeth instructed Mrs. Townsend to gather Mary's clothing and personal items and have them sent to Argyle. Before she'd left home, Elizabeth had told Edith to make ready the guest bedroom for Mary.

Now, Elizabeth sat with Mary in her arms, rocking in silence on the trip back to Argyle. Both women exhausted, silent. They sat staring out the window, looking at nothing.

Soon enough, the agony of their loss would be eased by focusing their hate on the man who had killed their husbands and ruined their lives forever: Henry Berry Lowrie.

CHAPTER 35

Word came to Henry Berry that the governor might reconsider his request for a pardon. But, the governor wanted to see Henry Berry and the members of the Lowrie Gang who wished to be considered for pardons, in-person. He wanted to hear from the gang members themselves.

Henry Berry wanted John Sanders, the Freedman Bureau's representative, to accompany the members of his gang and represent them as council when they met with the governor. However, Representative Sanders was on a trip back home to Boston, visiting his ailing mother. The gang would have to go by themselves. The trip would take them by train to Wilmington where they would meet with the governor's representative. Then on to Raleigh to present their case for a pardon.

When the gang members arrived at Wilmington Station, they were met by a young man who said he was from the Freedman's Bureau and would take the men to where the governor's agent was staying. The men arrived across town and were led into a brick warehouse and asked to wait while the governor's agent was told of their arrival.

As the men stood around mumbling to each other, all the doors connecting adjacent rooms opened, and armed deputies surrounded the group of Indians. They were arrested, handcuffed and taken to the Wilmington Jailhouse; an old three-story red brick building that was almost a hundred years old, but still solid and foreboding.

People bustled about the jailhouse; loved ones waiting to visit, lawyers moving from courtroom to courtroom, and prisoners being led away or brought to the jail.

The entrance door to the jail was thick oak with iron bars to close it securely. The jailer's office was located at the entrance and was the room everyone entered when entering or leaving the jailhouse. Beyond the jailer's office were rows of cells, each cell containing at least one prisoner. The second-floor cells were empty due to renovations having just been completed. The third-floor cells were also empty because improvements were about to begin.

The Lowrie gang members: George Applewhite; Calvin and Henderson Oxendine; Tom, Steven, and Henry Berry Lowrie were taken to the second floor. Each man was locked in a separate cell, and the cell door on the main floor was also locked. The men were left alone because the first floor was heavily guarded, and no one was breaking out through the front door alive. That much was certain.

After dinner, Tom Lowrie managed to sneak a spoon off his tray, and the theft went unnoticed. Tom was an amateur locksmith, and he'd convinced the jail deputy that searched his person that his small nail file was of no use, for it could not file through iron bars. The very thought made the deputy chuckle, and so Tom was allowed to keep his nail file. He was now using it to file the stolen spoon into the shape of a key to open the jail cell doors. He worked all through the night, and by the next morning, he had a working key. He could open and lock their cell doors at will.

Every hour, like clockwork, a deputy would come up to the second floor to ensure all the prisoners were in their cells and accounted for and all the cell doors were locked.

As soon as the on-watch deputy departed and was heard bolting the cell door on the first floor, Tom would use his spoon-key to unlock all the cell doors. One man would go about halfway down the stairs to listen for any sound that the first-floor jail door was being unlocked. Tom stood by the main jail door to the second-floor jail cells, and three men would go up to the third floor to a middle cell with one side being the outer wall at the back of the prison. Here, the men took out their own stolen spoons and started scraping away the soft white mortar that held the bricks together. They knew that old buildings were made of old technology and the mortar between the bricks was made of a mixture of potash, lime, sand, straw, and water, strong enough to hold bricks in place, but soft enough to be dug out with a metal spoon.

As soon as the sounds of keys being placed into a lock were heard on the first-floor door, the alert was given, and all the men quickly returned to their cells, Tom ensuring each door was securely locked before the deputy came by on his security check rounds. As usual, the deputy found the prisoners napping, playing solitaire, or playing a harmonica. The second floor was always peaceful.

After a full day's work, the Indians had carved out enough bricks so that even Steven's broad shoulders could squeeze through. That night, just after the last nightly security check, all the men went up to the third floor and brought their bed sheets with them. The sheets were twisted and tied tightly together to form a rope that they tied to the jail cell bars. The bedsheet-rope was long enough to extend out the hole in the cell wall almost down to the ground, three stories below. One by one, they climbed down the sheets.

Once everyone was accounted for, the men followed the shadows through alleys and backstreets until they were well north of the city. They figured any posse would likely search south and/or west, thinking the men would head straight home. Instead, they went north, then west, then south. It took them almost a month to finally reach the backwaters and swamp they called home.

The morning following the jailbreak, the first deputy to go to the second floor unlocked the main door to the second-floor jail cells. You can imagine his surprise when he found all the cell doors locked and none of the men present. It seemed as though the Indians had simply vanished!

After a frantic hour-long search of the first two floors, how the men escaped only became known when someone saw the rope of sheets hanging from outside the third-floor wall. It seemed no jail could hold Henry Berry Lowrie.

CHAPTER 36

When Elizabeth heard that the Lowrie Gang had been captured only to escape once more, she was incredulous! This was some sort of sick joke, right? They really didn't arrest the Lowries, now did they? But, the fact was, the Lowries had been arrested and had made their escape.

Such incompetence was unbelievable!

Of course, Elizabeth had to inform Mary of the news, which caused the women to spend the next few days plotting ways to hang Henry Berry Lowrie, or shoot him, and never give him a chance to escape ever again.

Their hatred could only be eased by one thing, knowing Henry Berry Lowrie was **DEAD**.

CHAPTER 37

Weeks of traveling and hiding kept Henry Berry from his family and his home. When he finally walked through the front door, he was met by his mother, Pollie, who introduced him to his new son, Henry Delany Lowrie.

Henry Berry cradled his new son in his arms and walked over to where Rhoda was sitting. She looked up and saw that he seemed to be glowing with his new son in his arms. Henry Berry sat down beside Rhoda, kissed her on the cheek, and told her she'd done him proud, again. Thank God, both mother, and son, and father were all well and free!

The next day, John Sanders arranged to meet with Henry Berry and talk about what had happened in his absence and what actions might be taken to stop the killing and bring peace back to Robeson County.

The idea John Sanders wanted to discuss was audacious. He was proposing that the Lowries, Oxendines, Locklear and Strongs, along with any Indians, poor whites and blacks that wished to leave to find a more peaceful home, pack up their things and travel, first to Georgia, where they would be resupplied for their journey, and then make the trip to the lands opening up in the far west.

Sanders said he had connections within the Freedman's Bureau that would guarantee their safety and see to it that they could resettle and rebuild a community away from all the bad blood flowing through Robeson County. He reminded Henry Berry that the Governor had raised the bounty for his arrest to $2,000. "If you stay in these here parts," Sanders told Henry, "someday someone will hunt you down and shoot you in the back. So, please, think of your wife and your family."

Henry Berry promised he'd talk with members of his community. He wanted Sanders to understand that he would not leave the helpless and the defenseless to go it alone against the murderous white Conservatives. Sanders pointed out that once Henry was dead, he could not defend or provide for his family. Maybe this is the right reason to leave their ancestral homelands, the chance to live in peace.

Adjusted for inflation
$2,000 of 1870 dollars
is worth **$36,614** in 2018

CHAPTER 38

On a cold December morning, a local white teenager, by the name of Henry Biggs, was up early hunting the woods for wild game. As he moved deeper into the swamp, he picked up the smell of a campfire on the wind. Following the smoke, he came upon a small camp where the previous night's fire was down to its last cinders. White smoke-wisps danced off the smoldering ashes to mix with the morning fog. Close by laid a white man, sleeping soundly. Henry Biggs crept up quietly, cautiously.

Once at the edge of the camp, Biggs was afraid to go any further. The sleeping man said something in his sleep and rolled over so that his face could be seen. It was Zachery McLauchlin, a poor white teenager, who was a friend of the Lowries. Because he was often seen with the Lowries, though he was never seen with them on a plantation raid, he had also been labeled an outlaw with a $200 bounty on his head, Dead or Alive.

Henry Biggs knew Zachery. The two teenagers were courting the same girl, and Biggs hated Zach because the girl seemed to be partial to Zach's company. While Zach lay there sleeping peacefully, Henry Biggs shot him through the left eye and once more in the chest, just for good measure. He then dragged the body back to Lumberton, where he collected his reward.

At the time, at an average worker's pay rate, it would take several weeks for a man to earn $200 ($3,661). So, for the teenager, Henry Biggs, it was not a bad day's pay. He couldn't help but feel proud.

CHAPTER 39

John Taylor was one of the county's wealthy men. He'd gotten rich by devoting vast amounts of his family's land to the production of tobacco, which required less labor and returned a higher per-pound dollar value than other marketable crops. Tobacco would someday be king and not cotton was John Taylor's prediction and he backed up his words with his vast fortune. He was a staunch Conservative, a community leader in his church, and a member of the KKK. He was also part of the firing squad that had murdered Henry Berry Lowrie's father and brother.

Taylor was of average height and thin. He had sad blue eyes, thinning blonde hair, and a full bright red beard. He had been a slave owner, as mean as they came. He believed the only way to get a black man to do an honest day's work was by intimidation and cruelty. However, when he was with "polite Southern Society," he was well dressed with impeccable manners and would flirt with ladies in a most heavily accented Charleston-style Southern drawl.

Few were fooled by this hypocrite and a lifetime of social snubs had left him bitter and mean. Losing the war and his labor force produced a great deal of pent-up anger, especially against freed blacks. He hated it when they acted "uppity," like they were HIS equal! How dare they!

His crutch and comfort in life had become whiskey. He'd try not to drink for most of the day but eventually his frustration at not feeling happy and his animosity toward a clear blue sky usually diminished his fortitude, and he would have his first drink of the day, well before noon. That first drink always lowered his blood pressure, turned his frown upside down, and his optimism would rise. By his fourth drink, he was as mean as a cornered dog with rabies.

One day, as he was riding home in his buggy, he came upon a black man and boy walking along the side of the road. When the two did not acknowledge Taylor's approach, he yelled, "Get out the road, you God damned nigger!"

The older man walking alongside the road was Ben Bethea, a freed slave who Taylor used to own. "I ain't your nigga no mo'," yelled Ben over his shoulder back at John Taylor, and he continued to walk along the side of the road, holding the boy's hand to keep him on the far side of the path.

"You think you somebody, now don't you? Well, you ain't shit. You got a job, yet? Now get the hell off my road, and you address me as 'Master' or, so help me God, I'll make you wish you had!" hissed Taylor through his teeth.

Ben and the boy continued walking alongside the road with their heads down. The little boy looked over his shoulder back at Taylor's buggy. Ben squeezed the boy's hand to regain his focus and look straight ahead. It was best not to look a drunken white man in the eye because they might think it was a challenge to their status and manhood.

Taylor persisted, "You gonna show me some respect? Or am I going to have to teach it to you, nigger? Now, get off my damned road!"

"I told you, I ain't yo nigga no mo. So, leave me be to go my own way. I'm a free man, and I have a right to walk where I please," said Ben firmly as he and the boy continued on their way.

"Okay, damn you, have it your way," stated Taylor, and he pulled his shotgun from the back of his buggy and shot Ben in the back, causing him to fall still holding the boy's hand. Miraculously, the boy was not hit. But he was terrified and stood frozen with fear. Taylor moved his buggy up beside the boy and said, "How are you going to address me, boy?"

To speak, the boy had to swallow hard before he could whisper, "Master Taylor, sir."

"Speak up, boy! What's that you said? Speak up!" shouted Taylor.

"I says I'd call you Master Taylor, sir," shouted the boy, who was so scared he pissed his pants.

"Well, now. You be sure and tell all your kind the proper way to address a white man. Ya hear? Now, you go home and tell your momma where this nigger's body can be found before it starts stinkin' up my road" stated Taylor, as he snapped his buggy whip between the horse's ears. The cart moved on with Taylor singing some song off-key. His mood seemed much improved by the encounter.

When Taylor's buggy had turned the corner and was out of sight, the little boy ran home to tell his momma what had happened. Hearing the news, she knew she'd not get justice from the local sheriff's office, which would simply rubber-stamp the murder as *Death by gunshot, not enough evidence to prosecute.* So, she turned to those who would help her get revenge on that murdering bastard, Taylor. She got word to Henry Berry Lowery.

Henry Berry knew John Taylor had been one of the men in the firing squad that had killed his father and brother. But he tried to give those men the benefit of doubt that they were only following orders. Therefore, Henry Berry chose not to pursue members of the Home Guard unless they moved to harm him or his family members and friends. Ben Bethea had been a friend.

A week after the killing of Ben, Henry Berry lay in wait behind a turkey-blind next to the road that led to John Taylor's house. Henry was waiting for Taylor. Taylor was not at home when Henry looked for him that morning. For nine hours, Henry Berry lay in wait for Taylor to come home.

Just before sunset, Taylor's buggy came slowly down the lane toward his home. He never saw Henry Berry. He only felt the hammer-blows of double-aught buckshot as they tore his chest apart, killing him almost instantly. At last, justice was served.

1871

Life is a goddamned, stinking,
treacherous game and
nine hundred and ninety-nine men
out of a thousand
are bastards.

Theodore Dreiser

Total documented raids on local plantations by the Lowrie Gang
in **1871 = 3**

CHAPTER 40

Tom Lowrie and one of the Oxendine brothers, Forney, were fishing early one morning a bit north of their usual spot. Today, they were trying their luck on a tributary of the Lumber River known as the Little Pee Dee River.

They'd been sitting on the bank for over an hour, and the fish didn't seem to be hungry. Perhaps a little piece of jerky they brought for lunch would be a better offer than the scrawny worms they were using.

Dropping the newly baited hooks back into the river, the men pushed the ends of their cane poles deep into the soft soil of the riverbank. All the men had to do now was be quiet and wait for the fish to bite.

To pass the time more comfortably, both men sat down and leaned back against sturdy trees, and were soon fast asleep. Their snoring was adequate to keep any curious fish far from shore. One thing an outlaw should never do is feel too comfortable.

Forney Oxendine was rudely jostled awake when he became aware of being kicked in the foot. He opened his eyes to see a slight-framed mulatto man pointing a rifle at his chest. Forney put his hands above his head. Might as well; his gun and Tom's were leaning against a tree close to where they had planted their fishing poles. Just enough of a distance to ensure neither outlaw could make it to their guns alive. Nothing left to do but surrender.

The man with the gun kept the barrel aimed at Forney. Then he kicked Tom Lowrie awake. Tom was no more rattled than Forney. He just yawned and said, "James, what do you think you're doing? Is this a joke?"

James McQueen, a local bastard-child who grew up in these swamps, had been a childhood friend of the

Lowries and Oxendines. He was a strange little man with beady eyes. He'd avert his gaze before anyone could lock eyes with him. The man was a sneak, a pickpocket, a liar, and usually lived like a hermit. But, the reward money for these two outlaws was too much and too easy to obtain to allow the opportunity to pass.

"Ya'll are my prisoners. Now get up and let's trek on over to the Maxton Jail," instructed McQueen.

By sunset, the men were in jail.

The next morning, word had reached the incarcerated men's families and soon the Lowrie matriarch, Pollie, was seen walking toward the jailhouse carrying a cake. She was dressed in a simple dress and had her hair pinned up on top of her head. She looked like most everyone's grandmother. She was an adorable little old lady.

Entering the jail's main door, she was met by the jailer, a local deputy who was on duty. He was alone, but with the town full of Union troops walking around, there was little chance of trouble.

"Good afternoon, deputy," said Pollie Lowrie as she closed the door behind her, appraising the obese man behind the desk.

"Good afternoon to you," said the deputy politely in reply, his eyes on the cake.

"I'm Pollie Lowrie, Tom's grandmother. Today is his birthday, and I want to give him the cake I made," Pollie said with a smile.

"Well, I'll have to cut it up first. You know, so I can make sure you didn't put a file or something inside," replied the fat man, only half-joking.

The deputy came around to the front of his desk and took the cake from Pollie. Focusing his attention on the cake and not Pollie, he sat it on his desk. Then, realizing his back was turned toward Pollie, his training kicked in, and he quickly moved around behind the desk, so he'd have a shield if needed. Pollie just stood, smiling, her hands holding her purse to her midsection.

"Just some small slices for my boys. That's a sweet bourbon pound cake. My recipe, something I call a Totten Cake. Not too much for my boys, I don't want them to get tooth problems."

She smiled in her most grandmotherly way. The deputy blushed and smiled back. No threats, here.

"How's that" asked the Deputy, indicating he wanted Pollie's approval at the size of the slices of cake.

"Why that's about perfect!" chimed Pollie, much to the delight of the deputy. She selected two slices and put a slice on two saucers. With each hand carrying a slice of cake, Pollie turned to follow the deputy toward the back of the building and the jail cells where Tom and Forney were being held.

As they neared the cell area, Pollie started singing "Happy Birthday to you." Surprisingly, the deputy piped up and sang along with gusto, because Pollie said he could have the rest of the cake for himself, news that brought a broad smile to his face.

The deputy would not allow Pollie to come in contact with either man. He didn't want her to give them anything they could use for an escape.

He did allow Pollie to walk near the cell bars so that she could give her grandson a happy birthday kiss. "That's a Totten Cake, Tom. I know it's your favorite. Happy Birthday, Tommy!" said Pollie. Her eyes fixed on Tom's; their gaze locked in communication as Pollie silently mouthed the words "don't eat the cake." Tom's eyes expressed he didn't understand because "totten," in their language, meant an unusual smell or sound indicating the presence of a demon. Understanding Tom's quizzical look, Pollie included, "This is my best recipe yet. Let's see, I put in flour, eggs, milk, a lot of honey, Sourbush leaves, and plenty of bourbon. I think you'll like it."

Hearing the ingredient "Sourbush leaves," Tom's eyes grew wide with understanding. Sourbush leaves were an old Indian laxative. His smile told Pollie all she needed to know. She then turned and smiled graciously at the deputy and walked away from the cell.

"Okay, that's it. Time to go. This way, Ma'am," indicated the deputy by extending his arm toward the door from which they'd entered. He followed Pollie toward the door, his mind already on that delicious looking cake!

Once the jail was again secure, the deputy took his place behind his desk and took his first bite of the cake.

"Why this is delicious!" exclaimed the deputy as he enthusiastically took another, bigger bite.

As Pollie shut the door behind her, she saw the deputy hungrily gobbling down the cake. Crumbs covered his shirt, and powdered sugar coated his mustache.

"Have a good evening," she sang out before closing the door.

"Mmm, thanks ...mnmmn da cake!" was the best the deputy could say in reply with his mouth full.

Just after dark, Henry Berry and a few of his gang made their way into the shadows across the street from the jailhouse where they could keep watch on the front door. Boss Strong walked a block further down the street to stables before moving into the shadows. Once stationed, he too, watched the jailhouse door.

Sometime just after 8:00 p.m., the jailhouse door was flung open, and the fat deputy stiffly shuffled around the corner of the building trying to run without separating his thighs. He held both hands behind his back and was trying to keep his butt-cheeks closed with a death grip. From across town, he could be heard yelling, "Oh no! Please, God no! No... NO... No! No! No! ......Ahhhhhh!"

When he reached the outhouse, he almost tore the door off the shed, and in a beautiful syncopation of body movements, he dropped his pants and slammed the door behind him. Moans, groans, farts and other assorted sounds emerged from behind the door, and then all was deathly silent. Even the night-creatures were dumbfounded and silenced by what they'd just heard.

Seeing the deputy leave the jailhouse was Boss Strong's signal. Unseen, he went into the corral, leaving the gate open behind him. He then puffed heavily on his cigar until the end was red hot. There was one horse, in particular, that seemed high-strung and skittish. Boss managed to move the horse so that it was pointed toward the gate he'd opened and plunged the red-hot tip of the cigar into the horse's ass. Its reaction was immediate and as predicted. That horse kicked-back, reared-up and bolted through the open gate and down Main Street away from the jailhouse. Boss ran out behind the panicked horse, yelling, "Whoa! Whoa! A little help here!!!! Hey?"

Everyone in town heard the commotion and saw the horse running loose. Men tried to spread their arms and yell "Whoa!" attempting to calm the beast or put a rope around its neck.

While everyone's attention was on capturing the horse, Steven Lowrie and Henderson Oxendine took up guard positions at each corner of the jailhouse.

Henry Berry walked to the jailhouse front door, pulled it open, and walked inside. A quick look around the room and he found the main key ring hanging on a peg behind the deputy's desk. He took the key ring, walked back to where the jail cells were and unlocked the doors to free his brother and cousin. Henry then closed and locked the cell doors. The three men walked out of the jailhouse and, together with Steven and Henderson, the group moved into the shadows to meet up with Boss. The group then walked unnoticed out of town and disappeared into the night.

CHAPTER 41

After much debate among his family and friends, it was decided the best hope for a new start was to just pack up and leave, as John Sanders had arranged, and be long gone before any pursuit could be organized.

The afternoon of the appointed exodus, Henry Berry was loading his possessions into his wagon. Rhoda packed, and Henry loaded. The plan was for all family members from the Lowries, Oxendines, Strongs, and Locklears to rendezvous after dark just west of Biggs Road and the bridge going over to Moss Neck.

Rhoda was coming out the house with a few kitchen pots, headed toward the wagon when she noticed a young Indian boy running toward them. She called to Henry Berry, who jumped off the back of the wagon, and the two adults waited to see what the boy had to say.

The boy was a blue-eyed Indian by the name of Everton Chavis. Out of breath from his long run, he said Edith, the Argyle house servant, had sent him with an urgent message. She'd overheard a conversation earlier that morning between Elizabeth McRae, Mary Norment, and John Sanders. They were discussing a plot to kill you all, and Miss Edith says you should *not* meet Sanders tonight to leave for Georgia. "She says, they plan to kill you all!"

Rhoda understood immediately and started to say something to Henry Berry. But she stopped short, for she could see something was stirring in him. She had learned long ago that when he became most calm and soft-spoken was when he was the most dangerous to those who threatened him or his family.

Rhoda remained quiet. Then, she walked back into the house, returning the kitchenware to their original locations.

Henry Berry just nodded and told Everton he was grateful to him for his bravery and to give Miss Edith his blessings and thanks. Everton's heart swelled with pride. Why, he was almost a hero and he smiled like one. His job complete, Everton turned and headed home with a skip in his step.

Henry Berry met Rhoda at the doorway and asked

her to unload the wagon while he went to spread the word to the rest of the gang members. He hugged her carefully because she was again pregnant and he reminded her that she should not try to lift anything heavy off the wagon. He would take care of those items as soon as he returned.

Just before sunset, Henry returned and took all the remaining items from the wagon before driving off to the agreed meeting site where John Sanders would lead them to "a better place."

Around midnight, the full moon was so bright that the only shadows in which to hide were found in the underbrush. The entire gang was present, and there were ten wagons lined up like a caravan, as John Sanders appeared riding up Deep Branch Road. Everyone waved back and forth, all friendly-like. Everything seemed to be ready as planned.

Sanders rode over to the lead wagon where Henry Berry was seated. When he came up to the side of the wagon, Sanders smiled broadly and said, "Looks like you guys are ready to go." Then he noticed that there were no women or children. Next, he looked behind Henry into the empty wagon. About the same time, he understood there was a change in plans when he saw that Henry Berry had a Navy Colt pistol aimed at his face.

"Get off the horse," ordered Henry Berry, with a great deal of authority in his voice.

Sanders dismounted and held his hands over his head and said, "I'm not armed."

To be sure, Boss Strong walked up behind Sanders and searched him for weapons. "He's clean," Boss said.

Henry motioned to Sanders to put down his arms, which he did. Henry uncocked his revolver and replaced it in its holster. He then led Sanders along a back trail to a secluded area not far from the river. A ways down the path a small fire could be seen glowing inside a circular clearing with log benches laying around its circumference.

After everyone was seated, Henry was handed a hot cup of coffee and he asked John Sanders if he'd care for a cup. Sanders was savvy enough from his experience as a Boston cop to know that during any negotiations it's best not to start on a negative note.

"I'd love some, thanks," Sanders said, hoping his smile looked genuine.

Everyone sat in silence as they waited for the hot cup of coffee to be delivered. No one wanted to be the first to start talking. A moment later and Sanders was sipping his coffee, "This is really good! One of your secret blends?" John asked, trying to start the conversation off with a light ring in his voice.

"John," began Henry, "I really liked you. In fact, I went against my better judgment and I trusted you."

"Now, Henry Berry, I don't know what has spooked you, but we need to have you south of Columbia before daylight," injected Sanders.

Henry didn't like being interrupted and he certainly did not tolerate being lied to.

"I know a great deal of what you have planned for us and I know you are in cahoots with the good folks over at Argyle."

"No! No! You don't understand. We.... I..." stammered Sanders.

But Henry impatiently held up his hand to signal Sanders to stop what he was trying to say and to just listen.

"Anyone who threatens me, my family or my friends, I'll see to it they die. Tonight, John Sanders is your last night on this Earth. Now, here's the deal. We have a tradition in these here parts that when a man is about to be executed, he should be allowed to write a final letter to his loved ones, on the condition that he tells us *truthfully* everything he knows. So, I want you to tell me everything you know. Starting with why you betrayed us. But take a moment to think about what you're going to say before you begin, because if you say something I know to be false, I'll kill you right here and now. Do I make myself perfectly clear, Mr. John Sanders?" stated Henry Berry, coldly.

John Sanders looked into Henry Berry eyes and could see the man was not kidding in the least. Before him sat a dangerous man, who would, no doubt, act on his words. Henry Berry's statement was not a threat but a promise, and he was known as a man who always kept his word.

Firelight flickered and made shadows dance across Henry Berry's face. Sanders couldn't be sure, due to the low light, but it appeared as though Henry Berry's normal sparkling blue eyes had turned as black as a shark's eyes. There was nothing there to see but death staring back at him. He felt a slight shiver run down his spine.

Henry left the Boston cop alone, under the watchful guard of his brothers, to allow him to consider the offer and consider his wife and three children. When Henry came back, John Sanders said he'd like to write one last letter to his wife and family. Then, he told Henry Berry everything.

His instructions from Argyle were to get the members of the Lowrie Gang to pack their wagons and leave Robeson County. They would travel south under cover of darkness, stopping for the first night just south of Columbia, South Carolina. Before moving on to Augusta, Georgia, instead of meeting up with their contact and guide, the caravan would be ambushed, and every man, woman, and child was to be killed.

John Sanders dropped his chin against his chest and sobbed loudly as he heard the words leave his lips. It was as though, for the first time, he understood the murderous gravity of the plan.

"I wish there was something I could do or say to change this night," Sanders said, tears running down his cheeks.

At Henry Berry's nod, Henderson Oxendine walked over to where John Sanders was sitting and handed him a pad of paper and a pencil. Steven Lowrie handed him a cup of brandy to calm his nerves.

While Sanders wrote the farewell letter to his family, Henry Berry and the other gang members held council to decide the man's fate. Boss Strong wanted to allow Sanders to go free on the condition he left the state and never returned.

Henry Berry was quiet for a long time. Then he said, "John Sanders is a traitor who was going to take us to slaughter. He must die." He then broke a small branch from a nearby tree and broke off enough twigs so each man could draw one from Henry Berry's hand. The man with the short stick was to execute Sanders. The man who pulled the short stick was Steven Lowrie.

Steven didn't want to kill Sanders, whom he liked, but, rather than make the job more difficult, he pulled his Navy Colt six-shooter from its holster and in one motion, leveled the gun at the side of John Sander's head and pulled the trigger.

Sanders made no sound. He fell over in a crumpled pile, dead.

The next day, the letter that John Sanders had written and addressed to his wife was delivered to the Moss Neck Train Depot where it was picked up by the mail train.

CHAPTER 42

Elizabeth and Mary seemed more upset by the news that their plot to execute the Lowries had been foiled than they were to hear that John Sanders was dead.

They immediately sent for James McQueen, the local Suffletonian bounty hunter, who had successfully captured Tom Lowrie and Forney Oxendine and assigned him the task of bringing in the members of the Lowrie Gang. The reward money was dumped on the table in front of McQueen so he could see how substantial the pile looked.

A week later, McQueen learned that George Applewhite's wife had given birth, and he knew George wanted to visit his home to see his wife and newborn. McQueen selected half a dozen Klansman to accompany him to sneak up, surround Applewhite's home and lie in wait for George to appear.

On the second evening of their surveillance, two men came walking down the lane toward Applewhite's house. They seemed unconcerned about a possible ambush and could be heard laughing at one of their quips.

As George Applewhite opened the front door to his home, he stepped aside to allow Henderson Oxendine to enter first. As Henderson moved to enter the house, James McQueen fired off a round hitting George Applewhite in his left arm, causing him to spin away from the direction of the shot.

On cue, the rest of the posse opened up and lead was flying, taking out chunks of the cabin walls and sending splinters flying from the front door. Applewhite was hit a second time, this time in the neck. He pulled his pistol and fired into the night toward the gun flashes assaulting him. He stumbled across the lane and disappeared into the blackness of the surrounding forest. All became quiet.

Not wanting to endanger Applewhite's family, Henderson Oxendine put a cloth over the end of a broomstick and held it outside the open doorway. "I surrender! Don't Shoot!"

McQueen answered by saying Henderson should come out, unarmed, with his hands up. Henderson came outside as instructed and was immediately frisked for weapons and handcuffed. The posse then marched off to deliver Henderson Oxendine to the sheriff in Lumberton.

The next day, the posse returned to George Applewhite's cabin expecting to find his body in the nearby woods. They found dried blood, evidence that Applewhite had been gravely wounded, but they couldn't find the body.

Elizabeth sent a telegram to the sheriff of Lumberton telling him that he would not allow this Lowrie Gang member to escape, *or else*. The threat was implied, but the lady had the connections, influence, and power to make the sheriff's life very difficult.

To ensure that Lumberton Jail's newest resident would not escape, the sheriff enlisted men of the old Home Guard, the local militia and members of the Ku Klux Klan to be stationed around the jailhouse at all times.

Four armed men were stationed outside Henderson Oxendine's cell where they could watch him around the clock. Additionally, Henderson was kept handcuffed, leg-shackled, and chained to the cell bars. He was one prisoner who would not escape.

The next day he was brought into court to stand before a judge. Henderson couldn't afford an attorney, but that was just a minor technicality.

The trial proceedings were a sham, and the judge declared Henderson Oxendine guilty of the murder of Sheriff Rueben King.

Henderson tried to tell the court that he had nothing to do with the sheriff's murder and that he was an innocent man. In response, the judge said Henderson was to be hanged at sunrise in two days, ensuring there would be no time to file an appeal.

Henderson Oxendine was outraged and the packed courtroom watched as the deputies had to physically carry the prisoner out of the courtroom, kicking and screaming, "I'm innocent you son of a bitch!"

The judge banged his gavel and shouted "Order in the Court! Silence!"

As the deputies pulled Henderson toward the exit door leading back to the jail cells, Henderson yelled at the judge, "Fuck You! You son of a bitch! Fuck You!"

The squad of deputies fought to remove the unruly, chained man. The judge, red-faced, yelled back at Henderson, "Put that man on bread and water for the remainder of his stay!"

"What?" shouted Henderson, "Fuck You!" And the guards finally managed to manhandle the prisoner out the door of the courtroom.

Someone in the back of the public gallery shouted, "Atta boy, Henderson!"

The exit door slammed shut, muffling the commotion on the other side. The judge hammered his gavel down and shouted, "Order! Order in the court! Silence!"

He slammed the gavel down so hard it broke, sending the head flying across the courtroom. He added, "If I find out who shouted that last outburst, I'll also give you thirty days in jail on bread and water!"

The courtroom became dead silent. The sight of the standing, robed, red-faced judge made it evident that the man was dead serious.

Calm restored, the judge regained his composure and sat down. Turning toward his deputy, he said, "Okay, what's the next case?" when the door where Henderson had exited burst open and Henderson jumped back into the courtroom, still in chains, and yelled at the judge, "...and fuck your wife, too!"

Hands appeared from the doorway and clamped over Henderson's mouth. More arms and hands appeared that grabbed him around his neck, shoulders, and waist. It was as though a giant octopus was attacking the man. Then, Henderson was lifted off his feet and again disappeared and the jail door shut behind him. The entire courtroom was stunned and silent. No one dared say a word for fear of the judge's wrath.

On the back row of the public seating area, two young Indians bent down behind the men sitting in the row in front of them so the judge couldn't see them. They locked eyes with each other, each boy smiling broadly and giving the thumbs-up sign, and silently mouthed the words, "Atta boy, Henderson!"

On the appointed sunrise, March 17, Henderson Oxendine was executed by hanging. His executioner, the man who pulled the lever to open the trapdoor beneath Henderson, was James McQueen, his abductor. For his part, McQueen collected a cash reward of $400. ($7,869).

That same evening, Rhoda Lowrie gave birth to her third child, a daughter they named Neely Ann Lowrie.

CHAPTER 43

Encouraged by the capture and execution of Henderson Oxendine, Elizabeth McRae and Mary Norment again petitioned the state governor to increase the reward on Henry Berry Lowrie, the focus of their hate. The governor agreed and upped the state's reward for Henry Berry to $10,000 Dead or Alive.

This amount of money was more than the average worker could hope to make in his lifetime! It brought to Robeson County an influx of bounty hunters, young and old, hoping to make their fortunes. After all, they were after just a few local Indians and only one man, in particular. Every bounty hunter held high hopes that he would be the lucky man to bring the outlaws to justice, *Dead or Alive* and collect the reward money. From then on, they would live on easy street.

For the remainder of the year, many bounty hunters went into the swamps and thick woodlands to find the outlaws. Few were ever seen again. It seemed those Indians just wouldn't fight fair.

One morning, Steven Lowrie was awake in his cabin and working on getting a fire going so he could make some coffee. As he was gathering his materials, he opened a window to let fresh air inside to take away the room's musty smell. As he turned to walk back to the fireplace, a breeze blew through the open window, carrying with it the scent of cigar smoke. Steven grabbed his shotgun and quietly walked out the cabin's back door and stealthily, swiftly made his way into the forest surrounding his house.

It had rained sometime during the night, which had soaked the ground and all the brittle leaves that had fallen were now soft and supple. Steven carefully made his way through the dense forest, his bare feet moving silently over the forest floor. He walked cautiously, gingerly placing his weight on one foot at a time. Each time he felt a twig underfoot; he lifted his foot and moved it to a spot that wouldn't make any noise. In this way, he silently walked through the forest until he saw a puff of white cigar smoke emerge from a thicket just beyond the front door of his cabin.

He positioned himself so he could see the back of a man's shoulders on each side of the tree he was sitting against. Steven approached the man's blind side, from behind the tree, unseen and unheard. The would-be assassin had been waiting all night for Steven to appear outside the front door of the cabin. The man was tired and bored. He leaned his head back against the tree trunk to watch the smoke rings he was blowing rise up and dissipate. It was a way to pass the time.

The man took a lengthy toke off his cigar and tilted his head back to exhale when he had a most peculiar sensation of quick pressure and a slight stinging across his throat. Somewhat absentmindedly, he reached his hand to his throat.

He brought his hand away from his neck and into view. For a moment, he was baffled and looked on in astonishment at the bright red blood covering the palm of his hand and flowing down the front of his shirt. Startled by the sight of blood, he jumped to his feet and stepped toward where his shotgun was leaning against a nearby tree.

He dropped his cigar and reached out to pick up his weapon. In horror, he felt a dark grey curtain close over his eyes. He fell face first onto the forest floor, unconscious, as his life bled out mixing with rainwater.

Steven placed his Bowie knife into its sheath and walked over and took the assassin's shotgun. He picked up the lit cigar, too. It had been a while since he'd enjoyed a good cigar. By the time he walked back to his cabin, the water for his morning coffee was bubbling angrily.

Adjusted for inflation
$10,000 of 1871 dollars
is worth **$196,733** in 2018

CHAPTER 44

The following month, Henry Berry and Boss Strong were spotted walking down a game trail, headed into the swamp. A group of seven bounty hunters on horseback gave the outlaws chase. As the bounty hunters rode onto the game trail, they managed to catch a glimpse of the two wanted men as they ran, taking a fork in the path about a hundred yards ahead. The men on horseback dug their spurs into their horses' ribs and raced to catch up.

When the horses made the turn at the fork, they again caught a glimpse of the fugitives as they rounded a corner further down the same path. The men on horseback faithfully followed the path around the corner and abruptly, pull up on their horses' reigns. The path ended in a cul-de-sac surrounded by a dense stand of sticker briar bushes.

Behind them, they heard a large tree fall. As the posse tried to turn their horses around to make their way out the way they'd come in, they found a large tree lying across their path with branches sticking out like spears. They were trapped. The outlaws opened fire with their Henry rifles, and in short order killed every one of the horsemen.

CHAPTER 45

A week later, another posse of bounty hunters, including a Cherokee Indian recruited from Georgia, followed Rhoda back to her and Henry's cabin. The next morning, the posse was in place in the woods surrounding the Lowrie cabin. They all waited for the signal to open fire.

Eventually, Tom Lowrie came outside and sat by the front door. He pulled out his fiddle and started to tune the instrument. Henry Berry, George Applewhite, and Rhoda could be seen inside the cabin. As luck would have it, Henry Berry's children were at their grandma's house for a few days.

Just as Tom drew the bow across the violin strings, the instrument exploded in his hands. For a brief moment, he was confused by what he'd done wrong. Then, the sound of a rifle shot reached his ears, and instinctively he dropped the violin and ran, ducking into the open cabin door, slamming it securely behind him. Shots rang out repeatedly, and bullets ricocheted off the cabin. The outlaws inside returned fire and managed to keep the posse at bay.

What the posse did not know was that when Henry Berry built his home, he took the precaution to construct a tunnel that led from beneath his fireplace, fifty yards underground to its exit at the river's edge. The outlaws, along with Rhoda, quickly made their way, unseen, through the tunnel and across the woods until they had flanked and surrounded the bounty hunters. They then ambushed the ambushers, killing five of the posse before the remainder of the men ran off into the surrounding swamp, never to be seen again.

It was beginning to seem that bounty hunters were becoming a daily nuisance. Times were becoming more dangerous by the day, and the outlaws had to constantly stay vigilant.

CHAPTER 46

"Damn it to hell!" hissed Elizabeth. "I brought you here to capture or kill the Lowrie Gang! You've been here now for over two months and what difference have you made? You came highly recommended by the governor, as a tracker, hunter, and buckskin from eastern swamp country and now you tell me you can't do the job? You mean to tell me you can't find enough men when the governor has again raised the reward to $20,000?"

Colonel Francis Marion Wishart, "Frank" to his friends, had to listen to his employer's exaggerated rants. He felt like telling the woman to go find the damned outlaws herself if she thought the task was so easy! But the lady did pay well, and Frank needed the money badly, so he allowed himself to be verbally abused, but only because the meeting was private.

"So," Elizabeth continued, "here are your orders. I want you to gather as many men as you need and I want you to arrest the wives of the outlaws. I want you to split your men into small squads and I want each squad to arrest one designated wife. I want you to time the raids so that each squad is at their assigned house at the same time. If you don't arrest all the wives at the same time, word will get out through the Indian's grapevine and any wife you've not yet arrested will be warned and you'll never find them. Only if you can capture all the wives will we be able to force Henry Berry and the rest of his gang to surrender. If they do not, their wives can rot in jail in their place."

The Colonel had to admit, these women were devious. Their purpose in life seemed to be the destruction of the outlaws, especially Henry Berry Lowrie. Frank had heard the stories and knew Henry Berry had murdered their husbands, and now they wanted their revenge.

"Mrs. McRae. Mrs. Norment. I give you my word your orders will be carried out successfully. We will have the wives under arrest before the end of the week. I promise you," swore Colonel Wishart.

"See to it that you do, Colonel. Now, good day, sir," Elizabeth concluded as she and Mary walked out of the room. They were the very model of defiance and control. Their wealth gave them power over ordinary men and they knew how to use it.

Two days later, Colonel Wishart had mapped out where the outlaw's cabins were located and groups of four or five men were each assigned a target. Their coordinated mission was successful and, by late in the day, all the wives were led off in a group as they began the long walk east along the Indian Highway that led to the Lumberton Jail.

The militia marched along with the wives in the middle of their column. The mission had been flawless and perfectly timed. Soon this mess would be done with and Wishart and his posse would be a great deal richer.

The men and women marched along uneventfully until Rhoda Lowrie seemed to step awkwardly on a rock that twisted her ankle. She fell to the ground. The other women rushed to her aid, and as they bent down by her side, a volley of rifle fire exploded from the woods on their left side. Three men in the posse were killed in the initial onslaught. Bullets whizzed overhead, and the men guarding the wives returned fire at Henry Berry and the other outlaws.

Henry Berry was concerned about the women and did not want to take the chance of hitting one by accident. So, as the posse pressed forward, the outlaws retreated into the woods hoping the white men would follow, which they did, guns blazing.

The battle was a running skirmish that moved deeper into the forest. The outlaws continued to move northward until they reached the banks of the Lumber River where they had stationed several flat bottom boats and a few canoes.

When the Indians reached a designated spot, four men stayed behind, firing their 15-shot Henry Repeater Rifles in rapid succession to keep the pursuing white men at bay while the rest of the gang ran to the river and paddled their crafts to the northern shore. There, the gang took up positions and waited for their remaining comrades to appear on the south side of the river. Of the three crafts left on the riverbank, the men used the last canoe to paddle across the river. They then quickly pulled their canoe over the embankment and established defensive positions behind trees and earth mounds. They reloaded their weapons and waited for their pursuers to appear on the south bank.

When the white men of the militia reached the south bank, they stood out on the open riverbank. When they saw the two flat bottom boats, several men in the group jumped into them and were pushed off into the river. They began to row feverishly in hot pursuit of their query.

No shots were fired until the bounty hunters were halfway across the water. Then suddenly, both boats came to an abrupt halt, throwing one man over the bow and into the water. The men still in the boats tried to paddle harder to get past whatever was halting their progress.

What they didn't know was that the Indians had planted those skiffs for the white men to take. Ropes were attached to the bottom of the boats that securely anchored the boats so that they could go no further than halfway across the river before the anchor lines pulled tight. At that moment, the outlawed Indians opened fire from the north bank and shot two of the four men in one boat and one of the three men still occupying the second boat. The men not shot quickly jumped into the river and swam underwater, as much as possible, in a desperate attempt to make it back to the south side of the river. Bullets struck the water all around the swimming men. The men who remained in the skiffs lay dying of their wounds.

Soon, the remainder of the men that had left the original group guarding the outlaw's wives were taking up positions on their side of the river. They began firing across the river into the woods where the Indians had taken their stand. The Indians returned fire.

The firefight kept up the rest of the afternoon and finally stopped when there was not enough light left to see across the river. The shooting slowly died out, and the woods became quiet again. The bounty hunters and militiamen set up a defensive perimeter and posted guards to watch the river.

Late in the night, one of the Militia guards thought he saw something moving down the river. As the object came downstream, it got close enough for the guard to make out what he was seeing. It was a canoe and the man paddling down the river was none other than Henry Berry Lowrie!

The sentry cocked his weapon, aimed and waited until Henry Berry was directly in front of him. Then, he fired a single shot. Henry Berry cried out as the canoe tipped over and he fell into the water.

"I got him!" shouted the excited sentry. "I got him! I shot Henry Berry Lowrie!"

The loud gunshot, along with the sentry's shouts of alarm, brought the rest of the posse to the riverbank and by the sentry's side. They could see the overturned canoe, but they couldn't see a body.

Some of the men quickly lit torches so they could see into the night. The group moved along the riverbank trying to peer into the dark waters around the canoe for any sign of the dead outlaw. One of the bounty hunters held his torch high above his head when an explosion erupted from behind the canoe. The bounty hunter was kicked back into the underbrush, a gaping hole in his chest where a load of double-aught buckshot had ripped through his body. He was dead before he hit the ground. In response, all the other men tossed their torches into the water.

Another shotgun blast exploded from the behind the canoe. This time, Henry Berry hit his second target in almost pitch-black conditions. Instead of the chest shot he intended though, the second barrel of his shotgun contained only birdshot that hit Jeffery Townsend in the right buttock. It was said that from that night on, Townsend shit BBs every morning for the next thirty years.

Panicked, the white men began to fire wildly into the water as they ran away from the river and disappeared into the woods. Most of them didn't stop running until they reached the Lumberton town limits.

Henry Berry was unharmed. But he understood that by this time, their wives had been taken by what remained of their guard-escort and would now be incarcerated in the Lumberton Jail.

Adjusted for inflation
$20,000 of 1871 dollars
is worth **$393,466** in 2018

CHAPTER 47

John McNair answered the knock on his front door, barefoot, dressed only in his work pants. Who could be at his door so early in the morning, he wondered? He opened the door and was most surprised to see Henry Berry Lowrie standing on his front porch, armed to the teeth with a pistol on each hip, a Bowie knife in his belt, two bandoliers full of bullets across his chest, a shotgun slung across his back, and a Henry rifle in his right hand. McNair stumbled back into his house as Henry Berry followed him inside, uninvited.

"Henry Berry," said McNair in a shaky voice, "you've taken most everything I have. I only have fifteen dollars left to my name, but you can have it," he said as he reached into his pants pockets and pulled out the cash and held it out toward the outlaw.

"You can keep your money, John," Henry Berry stated. "I'm here to ask a favor of you."

John McNair took another step back and squinted at Henry Berry as though it might help dissipate his confusion. "What kind of favor?" he asked.

"I don't write too good, and I need you to write a note for me. Colonel Wishart and his men have arrested our wives and are holding them in the Lumberton Jail. I humbly request you take a message to them for me and my friends. Will you do that for us, please?" he intoned most sincerely.

"Why, yes, I suppose I could do that for you. Arrested your wives, you say? For what? What did they do?" asked McNair.

"They ain't done a damned thing, which is the point. They have been arrested for no other reason than they are our wives," said Henry Berry in reply.

"I see," said John McNair, scratching his whisker-stubbled chin, considering what he'd just been told. "Sure, come on into the study and tell me what you want written," McNair finally said. He then turned and walked toward his library where his roll-top desk held paper and pen.

Later that afternoon, John McNair was knocking on the door of the Inn where Colonel Frank Wishart was staying. Wishart took the note, unfolded the paper. As he slowly read the note, all the color drained from his face. The note was simple and to the point:

If our wives are not released and sent home by next Monday morning there will be worse times in Robeson County than there ever has been yet. We will commence to drench the county in blood and ashes. We promise to make it so no white woman in the county will be safe.

Signed,

H. B. LOWRIE

STEVE LOWRIE

ANDREW STRONG

That evening, the outlaws' wives were set free.

4 *The Lowrie History*, by Mary C. Norment

CHAPTER 48

Colonel Frank Wishart arrived at Argyle Plantation the next day to report to Elizabeth and Mary. He knew the women were not going to be happy. But all he could do was explain that he had a wife and three children, and his first responsibility was to his own family. He was ready to walk away from the job.

Elizabeth knew Frank Wishart was one of the best bounty hunters in the business. If he couldn't get the job done, maybe no one could. But she and Mary would not even allow themselves to consider such a scenario.

"Well, Colonel, you carried out your orders. We believe you would have stood firm if the leaders in the community had not been so spineless in the face of such a thug. Therefore, Mary and I are going to match the state's reward of $20,000, and we'll give you until early next year to obtain the men you need to sweep through the swamp and kill Henry Berry Lowrie. We no longer wish to see the murderer given a chance to escape. Your mission and the mission of your men is **to KILL Henry Berry Lowrie**. We want this struggle to end and we implore you to get the job done. Is there any reason you cannot succeed when $40,000 is at stake?" asked Elizabeth.

"No, ma'am," Wishart replied, "that's a mighty handsome sum of money. No doubt we can get a significant number of men to join the hunt. I'll see to it that the word gets out. I think we can gather enough men and have our plans ready soon after the New Year if you can wait that long."

"Colonel, we'll wait till hell freezes over if it means we can spit on Lowrie's dead body." Mary, sitting beside Elizabeth, nodded her head in agreement.

It was settled. The mission was to sweep through the swamp, find Henry Berry Lowrie and kill him. The two women waved as Colonel Wishart rode away from Argyle, satisfied their wishes would finally be granted.

1872

Self-trust is the essence of heroism

Ralph Waldo Emerson

Total heists by Henry Berry and the Lowrie Gang
in **1872 = 2**

CHAPTER 49

Rhoda was well aware of the Conservatives plan to kill her husband. The word had quickly spread far and wide. Bounty hunters were coming into the county from as far away as Ohio. Who could resist such an astounding amount of money? The governor was offering $20,000, and Argyle was matching that bounty with another $20,000, which meant the total amount of reward money was $40,000 for Henry Berry Lowrie **DEAD!**

Worse, for all the non-whites, the Union troops left Robeson County and that meant law and order was again the jurisdiction of the Conservative Whites.

Rhoda and Pollie discussed the situation with Henry Berry and reminded him of his family, his children, and Rhoda's love. But, he wasn't sure what he could do. What he should do. Even if they all ran away to some other place, how could he provide for them when he had no money?

The only way he could get money for them to live would be to steal it. And, if he did that, no matter the new place they moved to, he would be labeled as an outlaw. Bounty hunters would be sent out again and, away from Robeson County, he'd have no family to turn to for help.

Rhoda tried not to allow herself to tear up, but *something* had to be done! *They were going to kill her husband,* if not this year, then the next. Someone was going to shoot him in the back and then where would his family be?

It was all too much for Henry Berry. He didn't start this war. He didn't want this war. All he ever wanted was to love Rhoda and raise a family. Why was peace so hard to find?

Finally, it got to the point that Henry Berry felt the women were nagging him and he needed some peace and quiet so he could think things through. He kissed his wife and mother, picked up his rifle and shotgun, put on his hat and walked out to find someplace to be alone. He was being backed into a corner, and he understood it was a death trap.

Adjusted for inflation
$40,000 of 1872 dollars
is worth **$786,931** in 2018

CHAPTER 50

February 19, 1872, was a bright, unseasonably warm morning. A crowd of bounty hunters, lawmen, ex-Confederate soldiers, members of the Ku Klux Klan, and just about any man with a gun and a need for fast cash were there for what was being called a Coon Hunt. All they had to do was track the prey, get the prey to run, and then KILL IT! What could go wrong?

Close to four hundred men from all parts of the country had gathered at the Lumberton Courthouse. Colonel Wishart was standing on the front steps of the Courthouse giving the men their final instructions. The plan was to send one group of men into the swamps from the west with the other group moving in from the east. The idea was that one or the other group would force Henry Berry Lowrie, or any other outlaws, to face one faction or the other. Both groups would employ dogs to run the Indians, just like hunting raccoons.

"Now, men," Wishart shouted so the men in the back of the crowd could hear him, "this hunt will prove to be the most lucrative job of your lives *IF* we can kill the outlaw, Henry Berry Lowrie. And *when we succeed*, each of you will immediately be paid in cash, in United States silver certificate dollars. Why, at this moment, the sheriff's safe holds the state's reward money of $20,000 ($393,466) which is a lot of money. However, the good people of Robeson County have decided to DOUBLE the reward to $40,000 ($786,931) to ensure we kill the man who has been terrorizing this county for *far too long*.

"Our good friends at Pope & McLeod Hardware Store have agreed to hold the additional reward money in their safe. So, make no mistake, the cash is here and each man will be paid his fair share just as soon as we bring back the body of Henry Berry Lowrie.

"Before we head out, I want to remind you that even though these Indians can't read or write, and don't seem real smart, I'm here to tell you they are cunning and *most intelligent*. So we all must stay alert and act smart! The man we most seek to kill is, Henry Berry Lowrie. You've all seen a sketch of his likeness. He's about five foot ten inches tall, lean, about 150 pounds. He has blue eyes, long black hair, and a bushy beard any of us would be proud to sport. He doesn't look it, but the man is a killer. My only order is for you to *be sure* you are killing the *right* man because there are a lot of Indians living in these swamps. Most of them are peaceful and we want to keep it that way. The last thing we want is a war with these Indians. And, if you aren't aware of why, these Indians just don't fight fair!

"I will offer you one tip because sometimes it's hard to tell an Indian apart from a white man at a distance. I suggest you take note of how they are standing, because a white man will lock his knees while standing. An Indian always keeps his knees slightly bent so he is better balanced and ready to pounce if needed."

One man, in particular, standing at the back of the crowd, listened intently. He made note to lock his knees when he stood. He was a most handsome man with sparkling mischief in his blue eyes and was one of the few clean-shaven men in that crowd.

The Lumberton sheriff stepped forward and said, "Men, we can get this killer! I won't call him an outlaw because *proper outlaws,* such as Jessie James, rob banks *not* defenseless widows. So, make sure your weapons are loaded and you take along extra water."

Eventually, the crowd saddled up and began to form into separate divisions. The blue-eyed man slipped back into the shadows behind the Lumberton Courthouse.

By noon, the bounty hunters were in position to begin their manhunt and they let their dogs off their leashes. Each man spaced himself about fifty feet apart from the man next to him as the line of men swept through the dense forest and swamp. Where there was water, the men used canoes to ferry themselves across, always keeping their lines as straight as possible.

The posse was deep into the swamp when nighttime fell, and soon, each man was pulling out his torch to light the way in order to continue their pursuit in the darkness. They would stay all night if they had too. They were going to kill Henry Berry Lowrie just as soon as they found him.

Sometime around midnight, off toward the east along the horizon, a glow in the night sky rose up from the direction of Lumberton. Someone shouted, "God damn it! The Lowrie's have set fire to Lumberton!" And the alarm was sounded.

As quick as the posse could, they left the forests and forgot about the Indian hunt and headed in the direction of Lumberton to help prevent the town from burning down.

It was first light the next morning before Colonel Wishart and the sheriff made it back to the Lumberton city limits. What they discovered was that most every **outhouse** in Lumberton had been set ablaze and the townspeople were still putting out fires. There was no real threat that Lumberton would burn as Columbia had when Sherman came through on his historic visit.

Most of the townspeople were milling around that morning, and it seemed everyone had their own opinion about the "Great Lumberton Robbery." Some thought they knew WHEN it was done. Some thought they knew HOW it was done. And, even though there were no witnesses, it seemed they all agreed on WHO had done the deed.

But the thing that hurt them the most was the truth and there was nothing they could do about it. The safe from the Sheriff's Office and the safe from the hardware store were both lying open in the middle of Elm Street.

CHAPTER 51

Not only did Henry Berry Lowrie steal his own reward money of $40,000 but the hardware store's safe had held an additional $2,000 of the store's on-hand cash.

In one night, Henry Berry Lowrie had managed to steal $42,000 (**$826,278**).

He likely wondered if the sheriff would now consider him a *proper outlaw* and not *just a thief*.

It really didn't matter though, because, after
February 19, 1872,
neither the reward money

nor   Henry Berry Lowrie

...was ever seen in North Carolina, again.

And that's documented historical fact!

The End

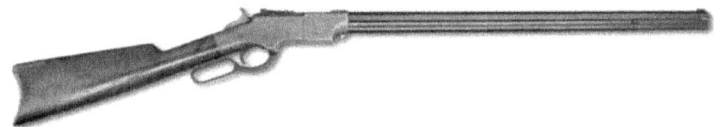

AFTERWORD

March 1872

Boss Strong was home on a Thursday night having dinner with his wife and brother, Andrew. After dinner, Boss began playing his harmonica, and Andrew sang along. With the outlaw's guard down, the bounty hunter James McQueen crept up to the cabin's front door and quietly pushed the barrel of his rifle through the small cat door at the bottom and shot Boss in the head. Not wishing to be confronted by Andrew, McQueen ran back to Shoe Heel. The next day, he contacted Colonel Wishart, and they gathered a posse and rode back to Boss Strong's home. The posse could not find Boss's body. His wife and his sister Rhoda would not disclose its whereabouts. Without a body, the sheriff was reluctant to pay the bounty on Boss Strong's head. After a year had passed and there was still no sign of Boss Strong, James McQueen was finally paid his bounty of $6,000 ($118,039). He then quickly left the state, never to return.

May 1872

F. M. Wishart set up a meeting with Steven Lowrie near the old Hope Baptist Church. No one knows what happened that day. But, the white citizens said Steven ambushed Wishart and killed him in cold blood. The Indians said it was Wishart who sprang a trap and Steven killed him in self-defense. The truth is, the truth will never be known.

July 1872

Thomas Lowrie was a man of habit. After opening a back window to pee out of, he moved over to his fireplace to start a fire. Smoke would soon begin to appear from the chimney around 8:30 a.m. – it was the same routine as most mornings. Given time for water to boil and his coffee to brew, Tom was usually walking out his front door by about 9:00 a.m. Unfortunately for Tom, the bounty hunter hiding in a blind outside the cabin that day did not smoke a cigar and Tom was shot through his heart. His killer collected a bounty of $6,200 ($121,974).

December 1872

Andrew Strong was drinking with a few friends on Christmas Day in the nearby town of Eureka. While there, they stopped in front of the John Humphrey General Store to say hello to some folks they knew. With his back to the store, Andrew didn't realize that William Wilson, the store clerk, had picked up a double-barreled shotgun. Wilson took careful aim and blew the back of Andrew's head off. William Wilson collected a bounty of $5,000 ($98,366).

February 1874

Steven Lowrie had become a recluse after his request for a pardon was again denied. Finally, the isolation became too much for him, so he ventured out to join friends around a campfire, enjoying a cookout. As the afternoon light faded, those who were musicians began to pick up their instruments to join in the festivities. Steven picked up a banjo and began a fast-paced, happy tune that caused those not playing an instrument to get up and dance. In the shadows, three young white men from Shoe Heel made their way through the brush until they could see Steven clearly. On cue, the bounty hunters opened fire and Steven fell under a hail of lead. He was dead before the music stopped. The other Indians around the camp ran off into the woods, fearing they would all be shot. The killers dragged Steven's body back to where they'd left their wagon and hauled the dead man to Lumberton. Steven's killers collected a bounty of $4,800 ($100,427).

July 1874

John McNair was paid $2,000 ($41,844) by Rhoda Lowrie as payment for all the times he had been robbed. He was a good neighbor and Rhoda insisted she provide him compensation for his stolen goods. Her generosity allowed him to pay back taxes and keep his farm from being appropriated by carpetbaggers. He also understood it was best not to ask where she got the money.

July 1874

Edith Argyle, Miss Betsy's house servant, somehow came into a "bit of cash" soon after Henry Berry Lowrie disappeared. Rumor has it that in short order she left Argyle for good. The last anybody heard, she'd found her daughter in Tennessee where she'd been sold by Master McRae. As far as anyone knows after that, Edith lived out her life with her daughter and her family

April 18, 1907

Elizabeth McRae, Passed away in bed, age 83, after weeks of complications due to "old age and heartache."

March 17, 1911

Mary Norment left Argyle Plantation soon after Elizabeth's death. She is reported to have moved to Charleston, where she lived out her days.

In 1909, she published,
The Lowrie history:
as acted in part by Henry Berry Lowrie

.

RHODA

In 1908, a young New York City reporter heard this story and traveled to Robeson County, North Carolina, to see if he could learn more. Eventually, he found a few Indians who would talk about the Lowrie War.

To his great delight, he learned that Rhoda Strong Lowrie, Henry Berry's wife, was still alive and still living in the county. He was told that after the Great Lumberton Robbery, when the money and Henry Berry disappeared, it was known that Rhoda would also disappear for weeks at a time, only to reappear looking refreshed, satisfied and happy. Though she'd never say where she'd been, rumor was that she traveled out west to see Henry Berry, likely in Tennessee.

It was only after much pleading and many payoffs that the reporter made the personal connection he needed. Arrangements were made and one Sunday, after church, he was introduced to Neely Ann, Rhoda's youngest daughter. At first reluctant, she eventually agreed to take the reporter out to see her mother. Rhoda Lowrie's cabin was located far off the beaten path, deep in the woods by the banks of the Lumberton River.

On the ride out into the country, with Neely Ann as his passenger, the reporter tried to make idle conversation. He wanted to know how he should act around Rhoda. Should he call her Rhoda or Mrs. Lowrie? Would she be okay talking about the old days? What could he say to make her feel more comfortable and talkative? But Neely Ann had a bad habit of staring straight ahead and not listening.

When the cabin finally came into view, the reporter reached over and touched Neely Ann's arm so she'd look directly at him as he implored her to clue him in, "How should I address your mother, Neely Ann?"

"Well now, I have to remind myself that you ain't never met my momma," replied Neely Ann. "All I can say is, just ask your questions. I have no doubt she'll have a reply."

As the old beat up Ford rattled to a halt under a shade tree near the cabin's front steps, the door to the cabin opened and a frail but handsome woman, even at such an advanced age, walked onto the porch. She sat down in her rocking chair and waved a *hello*. Then indicated they were welcome to join her on the porch.

Neely Ann introduced the two and then politely excused herself, entered the cabin, and closed the door behind her.

The young reporter tried to get on Rhoda's good side with a little flattery. "Mrs. Lowrie, it is such a privilege and honor to meet you. And, I must say you look so young for your age!" he said, smiling broadly.

Rhoda grinned an almost toothless smile and quickly had to grab her corncob pipe before it fell into her lap. "Thank you. That's mighty kind of you, but it's a damn lie, so git to your point."

Rattled, the young man told Rhoda the story of the legend of Henry Berry Lowrie, as best as he'd been able to put it together from his research. The whole time he couldn't tell if the old woman was listening to him or was lost in a different time and place. She just looked far off toward the horizon and puffed on her pipe while rhythmically rocking her chair, stopping occasionally to spit a brown wet wad of tobacco juice over her shoulder and onto the grass.

When the reporter had finally finished his tale, he asked her, "Is what I've recounted true?"

Rhoda just kept staring, rocking, and puffing on her pipe while she contemplated the question. Finally, she said, "Yep, pret' near."

The reporter was starting to think his trip might have been a waste of time, so he naively asked, "Why did Henry Berry only rob the rich white plantations?"

"Well, because they could buy more items to replace what was stolen. Hell, why would he rob the poor? They don't got nothing to steal," added the wizened old woman, realizing the inexperience and depth of this young man's stupidity.

Embarrassed and frustrated, the reporter went straight to the matter at hand and asked, "Do you know what Henry Berry did with all the money he stole? Did he bury it around here or did he take it with him when he left? For that matter, where did he end up?"

Abruptly the chair stopped rocking, and Rhoda said, "Now, that's personal." Then she gathered herself together, stood up, and walked to the front door of the cabin, and started to go inside.

The reporter quickly called out, "Please, Mrs. Lowrie, tell me something about your husband that I can put in the newspaper and tell the world."

The desperation in his voice caused Rhoda to pull up with one foot inside her house and the other still on the porch. She pondered the question for a moment, took a deep breath, and after letting out a long sigh, looked again toward the horizon, into the past.

"Okay, I'll tell you what to print. And this is the truth. Henry Berry Lowrie was a peace-loving man, a good man, a man who always kept his word and did what he said he was gonna do. He told everyone that he would leave them alone if he and his family was left alone. He only killed men that needed it, men that caused harm to his family or hunted him like a wild animal for the bounty money. He never harmed a woman or child. He never burned down no one's home. He never hung nobody."

Then she turned toward the young reporter and looked him directly in the eyes. For an instant, he noticed her eyes were all twinkly as she added, "Henry Berry Lowrie was the finest looking best example of a man I ever laid eyes on."

Then she spit tobacco juice across the young reporter's new shoes and said, "Now git the hell off my porch."

She then stepped inside her cozy little home and softly closed the door behind her.

TIMELINE OF EVENTS

January	**1865**	John McNair **PLANTATION RAIDED**
January 15	1865	Fort Fisher falls to U.S. Forces
January 15	1865	Brantley Harris **KILLED by Henry Berry Lowrie**
February 15	1865	Robeson County Courthouse at Lumberton - guns & ammo taken **PLANTATION RAIDED**
February 1	1865	Mrs. Martha Ashley **PLANTATION RAIDED**
February	1865	David Townsend, Esq. **PLANTATION RAIDED**
February	1865	Robert McKenzie, Esq. **PLANTATION RAIDED**
February	1865	Douglas McCullum **PLANTATION RAIDED**
February	1865	Henry Bullock, Jr **PLANTATION RAIDED**
February 27	1865	**Argyle Plantation** **PLANTATION RAIDED**
February 28	1865	Daniel Baker **PLANTATION RAIDED**
February 28	1865	McKay Sellers **PLANTATION RAIDED**
March 3	1865	Calvin Lowrie & William Lowrie arrested for "stealing/hiding" food and guns. **WILL** **– ESCAPES & RE-CAPTURED**
March 3	**1865**	**Alan & William Lowrie** **"TRIED & EXECUTED"**
March 5	1865	Calvin Lowrie **RELEASED**
March	1865	Indians dig up dead men, wash, dress and provide a "decent burial" on their land

March 9	1865	U.S. General T. Sherman **crosses Lumber River**
April 1	1865	20 men of Home Guard arrest & **"MOCK EXECUTED"** Mary Cumba "**Pollie**" Lowrie (Henry Berry Lowrie's mother)
April 9	**1865**	**Lee surrenders** **war is over**
April 14	1865	U.S. President Lincoln **SHOT**
April 15	1865	U.S. President Lincoln **DEAD**
April 15	1865	Home Guard becomes **KKK** secret military association
May 1	1865	H. G. William Humphreys & gang William Locklear & Hector Oxendine **ARRESTED**
May 10	1865	Confederate President, Jefferson Davis **ARRESTED** ***WEARING A DRESS**
March	1865	Joseph Thompson **PLANTATION RAIDED**
May 15	1865	The **13th** Amendment (Amendment XIII) to the United States Constitution adopted. Lumberton "town crier" announces all slaves henceforth are *FREED!*
June 21	1865	President Johnson removes U.S. General Joseph Roswell Hawley - a radical (Liberal) Republican commander of the military district of Wilmington with a *Conservative.*
August	1865	Former Confederate Colonel James Sinclair appointed to sever as Lumberton Freedman's Bureau - he also helped blacks organize a church of their own in Lumberton

October 16	1865	Plantation owner Willis Moore - shoots Patrick Barnes, a black servant for "stealing corn"
September 16	1865	Lumberton Mayor Charles J. Wickersham received a petition from the "citizens of Robeson County" (Conservative Whites) to remove Col. James Sinclair from the local Freedman's Bureau at Lumberton for the reason that "he has been obnoxious to the people (whites)"
	1865	Conservatives look to gain the upper hand
1865 thru	**1866**	**Era of presidential Reconstruction**
March	1866	Conservative Governor Jonathan Worth offers **Reward** **Henry Berry Lowrie** **$300**
November	1866	Daniel Baker shot
December 7	1866	**Henry Berry Lowrie** **MARRIES** **Rhoda Strong**
December 7	1866	Home Guard Lieutenant A .J. McNair - arrests Henry Berry Lowrie for the murder of J. P. Barnes **ESCAPE** #**1**
April	**1867**	**Henry Berry Lowrie** **first born** **Sally Ann**

May	1867	Radical (Liberal) Bureau agents began investigating the killing of certain Indians (Lowries & Oxendines)
June	1867	John McNair **PLANTATION RAIDED**
Spring Term	**1868**	When "Indian killing cases" came before the court - the Conservative Prosecutor wrote "Nolle Prosequi" across each indictment, indicating the State did not choose to prosecute the Home Guard.
March	1868	Lowrie Gang discontinued plantation raids on Bakers, McNairs, Townsends & other families of the Home Guard - which began when Gov. Worth outlawed Henry Berry Lowrie
January 23	1868	John McNair **PLANTATION RAIDED**
July	**1868**	**End of Reconstruction** **MILITARY LAW ENDS**
	1868	Conservatives lost control of all LEGAL means for inflicting violence upon their enemies and for protecting property, including courts, militia & police.
July 9	1868	The **14th** Amendment (Amendment XIV) to the United States Constitution adopted. All U.S. Citizens are of Equal Rights.
October 10	1868	Governor Holden got a letter from J. W. Schenck, Jr., Republican sheriff of New Hanover County - asking if the $300 reward for Henry Berry Lowrie put forth by his predecessor Conservative Gov. Jonathan Worth was still valid.
October 20	1868	"Indians" raided the plantations of Elizabeth Carlisle, James H. McQueen, Alexander McKenzie - all in Robeson County

November 30	1868	Governor Holden issued a proclamation of Outlawry against Henry Berry Lowrie and his followers
December	1868	Local Republicans attempted to negotiate a compromise - set a meeting between Henry Berry Lowrie & Dr. Alfred Thomas. Sheriff Benjamin A. Howell (replace Reuben King's 18-year reign as Robeson County Sheriff.
December 12	1868	**Henry Berry Lowrie** **SURRENDERED** to Debtors Jail in Lumberton -- Dark rumors swept from cabin to cabin along the Lumberton River and finally reached Henry Berry Lowrie in the debtor's cell. He grew suspicious and uneasy. **ESCAPE** # **2**
January 23	**1869**	Former Sheriff Rueben King **MURDERED**
April	1869	Richard Townsend **PLANTATION RAIDED**
May	1869	David McKellar **PLANTATION RAIDED**
May	1869	Henry Bullock, Senior **PLANTATION RAIDED**

Black Codes of N.C.	1869	"Persons of color contracting for service were to be known as 'servants,' and those with whom they contracted, as 'masters.' On farms, the hours of labor would be from sunrise to sunset daily, except on Sunday. The negroes were to get out of bed at dawn. Time lost would be deducted from their wages, as would be the cost of food, nursing, etc., during absence from sickness. Absentees on Sunday must return to the plantation by sunset. House servants were to be on call at all hours of the day and night on all days of the week. They must be 'especially civil and polite to their masters, their masters' families, and guests,' and they in return would receive 'gentle and kind treatment.' Corporal and other punishment were to be administered only upon order of the district judge or other civil magistrate. A vagrant law of some severity was enacted to keep the negroes from roaming the roads and living the lives of beggars and thieves."
March 19	**1870**	Home Guard Leader O. C. Norment murdered
February 3	1870	The 15th Amendment (Amendment XV) to the United States Constitution prohibits the federal and state governments from denying a citizen the right to vote based on that citizen's "race, color, or previous condition of servitude." * The third and last of the Reconstruction Amendments.
April 21	1870	John Purnell **PLANTATION RAIDED**

May	1870	Zach Fulmore **PLANTATION RAIDED**
June 12	1870	Rhody (&Henry Berry Lowrie?) go to Wilmington to breakout Stephen Lowrie, George Applewhite, Calvin Oxendine, Henderson Oxendine **ESCAPE** # **3**
July	1870	David Townsend, ESQ **PLANTATION RAIDED**
August	1870	James D. Bridges **PLANTATION RAIDED**
August 4	1870	E. H. Paul **PLANTATION RAIDED**
October 4	1870	The Old Field Fight aka: Brandy Wine **PLANTATION RAIDED**
October 8	1870	J. Taylor **MURDERED**
November 21	1870	John Sanders - detective **EXECUTED**
November 30	1870	Mrs. William McKay **PLANTATION RAIDED**
November	1870	David Townsend, ESQ. **PLANTATION RAIDED**
September 12	1870	Alexander McMillan, Esq. **PLANTATION RAIDED**
December	1870	State legislature offered **Reward** **Henry Berry Lowrie** **$2,000**

February	**1871**	State legislature offered ## Reward **Henry Berry Lowrie** ## $10,000
February	1871	John McNair **PLANTATION RAIDED**
February 26	1871	Henderson Oxendine **HUNG**
April 21	1871	Lowries escape ambush on their cabin by **escape tunnel** **ESCAPE** # **4**
May 10	1871	Tom Lowrie and Forney Oxendine **ARRESTED**
June	1871	Henry Berry Lowrie & gang break out Tom Lowrie and Forney Oxendine from the fortress-like - entered the jail by means of a key - unlocked the cells - broke off the irons - and locked the cells & front door when they left **ESCAPE** # **5**
July 8	1871	John McNair LAST **PLANTATION RAIDED**
July 10	1871	F. M. Wishart comes to hunt Henry Berry Lowrie Gang
July 10	1871	Outlaws **WIVES** **JAILED**
July 10	1871	Fight at Wire Grass Landing
July 14	1871	John McNair - asked by Henry Berry Lowrie to write a letter to free wives

July 14	1871	Lowrie Gang member's wives **are all set free**
December	1871	Angus S. Baker **PLANTATION RAIDED**
January	**1872**	State legislature offered **Reward** **Henry Berry Lowrie** **$20,000**
February 19	1872	**Great Lumberton Robbery** Store & Court House Safes * reward money is stolen **Henry Berry Lowrie Disappears ESCAPE** # **6**
March 6	1872	Boss Strong **MURDERED**
May 16	1872	F. M. Wishart **MURDERED**
July 15	1872	Thomas (TOM) Lowrie **MURDERED**
December 25	1872	Andrew Strong **MURDERED**

HISTORICAL NOTE

January 1966 was a time of high racial tension as the country became desegregated by way of the Civil Rights Act, signed into law by President Lyndon Johnson in 1964. It was a time of racial riots in most states across America.

The Knights of the Ku Klux Klan of North Carolina decided it would be a good idea to hold a revival and recruitment drive for new members from the Conservative whites living in Robeson County. The Klan advertised heavily and leased some land outside the town of Maxton, out by the swamp.

The night of the rally, more than fifty Klansmen arrived with their families, expecting to put on a good show. The Klansmen wore their white sheets and matching dunce hats. A portable generator was brought along to supply power to light the stage.

Finally, it was time for the event to begin. As the speakers approached the stage, a caravan of cars pulled into the field where the event was being held. It seemed to the Klansmen that the evening was going to turn out to be a big success. However, when the new arrivals got out of their cars, they turned out to be about three hundred heavily armed Robeson County Indians who were not there to welcome the KKK into their County.

When the leader of the Klan stepped up to the microphone and opened his mouth to speak, someone in the crowd shot out the light hanging above his head. Then, all hell broke loose and shots were fired from every direction. Fistfights broke out and the Klansmen were overwhelmed. As a last resort, they ran off into the safety of the swamps.

Order was restored. The Indians allowed the Klansmen's women and children to drive home, unharmed.

Over the next two weeks, the Klansmen began to find their way out of the swamp and the Indians gave them rides home after suggesting, in no uncertain terms, that the Ku Klux Klan was **not** welcome in Robeson County.

Fortunately, no one was killed. But the Indians made it known that they would not tolerate the hatred of white supremacists.

This, too, was a legacy of Henry Berry Lowrie and his gang.

INTO THE 21ST CENTURY

Today, Pembroke, North Carolina (The Settlement) is a thriving town where the educational efforts of their Indian Council have paid off. The town is built around the campus of the University of North Carolina, Pembroke (Once known as Pembroke State College for Indians).

The population of Robeson County is more than eighty percent Native American (Indian), and most residents have their undergraduate degrees from the University of North Carolina, Pembroke Campus.

Robeson County, North Carolina, is one of the few remaining places where you can still find *Real Americans* - **Native Americans** – perhaps, descendants of the Lost Colony - that still speak with an Old English brogue.

This is **their land**, the resting place of their ancestors;

...the land of the free and the home of the brave.

Cain't nobody make you feel inferior without your permission.

Pollie Lowrie

Henry Berry & Rhoda Lowrie's Home

Their cabin was restored and is now located at the *Strike at the Wind* Outdoor Drama, Recreation Area just west of Pembroke, N.C.

Highway Historical Marker on U.S. 74-Alt. in Robeson County, N.C.

Rhoda Strong Lowrie
(aka: Lowry; Lowery)
Died October 18, 1909
Harpers Ferry Baptist Church Cemetery
Robeson County, North Carolina, USA

ABOUT THE AUTHOR

Reader's Favorites presented their prestigious <u>5-Star Award for Excellence</u> to Warren R. Reichel, for his novel,

WANTED DEAD

The Legend of Henry Berry Lowrie.

Warren R. Reichel is originally from Richmond, Virginia and is a graduate of Virginia Commonwealth University with a B.S. in Mass Communications.

His unique insights and historical viewpoint grew from his family's relocating every few years.

About living in Richmond, the capital of the Confederate States of America, he notes that, "You can't throw a stick without hitting something to do with the Civil War in and around Richmond."

His family moved to Charlotte, North Carolina where he attended school in Mecklenburg County, just north of the South Carolina border and less than 90 miles west from where the events in this book took place.

When not writing novels and screenplays, Mr. Reichel is a humorist.

Coming soon....

As the Nazi War Machine grinds to a halt in Stalingrad, in Heidelberg, a young female journalist and British Citizen is arrested by the Gestapo and placed under intense interrogation – accused of being a <u>British SPY</u>!

Her husband, a Nazi S.S. Colonel, steps in to defend his wife and is arrested – accused of <u>TREASON</u>!

What could go wrong?

<u>The Spy of Heidelberg</u>™

Another gripping tale **based on**

TRUE EVENTS!

Mrs. Janet "Zoe" Schmitt

Colonel Fredrich Heinrich Schmitt

Also coming soon....

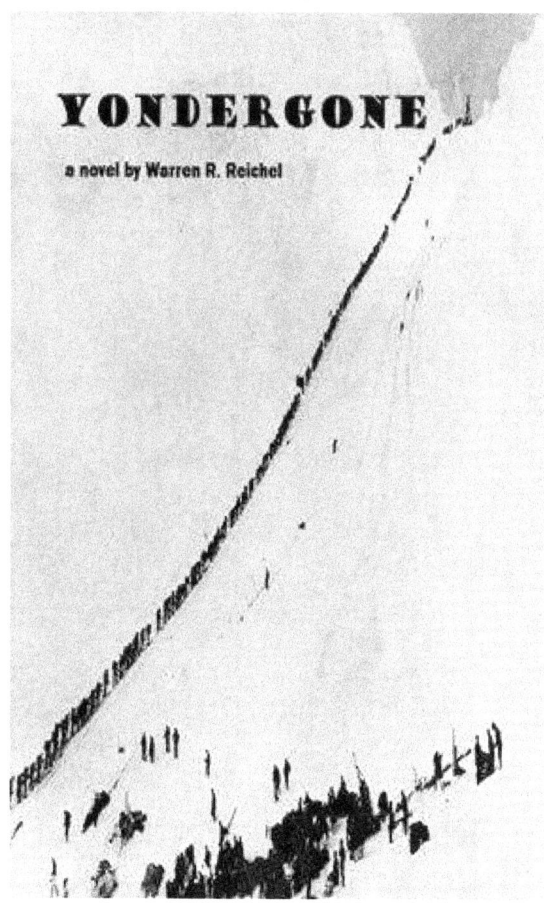

Yondergone™

– the story of a western dirt-farming family that gets Gold Fever and travels to the Yukon Territory to seek their fortunes.

Books available in

PAPERBACK
And
KINDLE